summer of yesterday

summer of
yesterday

Gaby Triana

SIMON PULSE

NEW YORK   LONDON   TORONTO   SYDNEY   NEW DELHI

This book is a work of fiction. Any references to historical events, real people, or real places are used fictitiously. Other names, characters, places, and events are products of the author's imagination, and any resemblance to actual events or places or persons, living or dead, is entirely coincidental.

SIMON PULSE

An imprint of Simon & Schuster Children's Publishing Division

1230 Avenue of the Americas, New York, NY 10020

First Simon Pulse paperback edition June 2014

Text copyright © 2014 by Gaby Triana

Cover photographs copyright © 2014 by Thinkstock

All rights reserved, including the right of reproduction in whole or in part in any form.

SIMON PULSE and colophon are registered trademarks of Simon & Schuster, Inc.

For information about special discounts for bulk purchases, please contact

Simon & Schuster Special Sales at 1-866-506-1949 or business@simonandschuster.com.

The Simon & Schuster Speakers Bureau can bring authors to your live event. For more information or to book an event contact the Simon & Schuster Speakers Bureau at

1-866-248-3049 or visit our website at www.simonspeakers.com.

Book design by Regina Flath

The text of this book was set in Centaur MT Std.

Manufactured in the United States of America

10 9 8 7 6 5 4 3 2 1

Library of Congress Cataloging-in-Publication Data

Triana, Gaby.

Summer of yesterday / Gaby Triana. — First Simon Pulse hardcover edition.

p. cm.

Summary: As she struggles with her parents' divorce, seventeen-year-old Haley is mysteriously transported to a theme park in the past, where she finds love and meets her teenaged mother and father.

[1. Time travel—Fiction. 2. Parents—Fiction. 3. Divorce—Fiction. 4. Love—Fiction. 5. Walt Disney World (Fla.)—Fiction.] I. Title.

PZ7.T7334Su 2014

[Fic]—dc23

2013045353

ISBN 978-1-4814-0130-2

ISBN 978-1-4814-0131-9 (eBook)

Yesterday is gone.
Tomorrow has not yet come.
We have only today.
Let us begin.

—Mother Teresa

one

A long time ago, in a water park far, far away, a boy and girl met, became friends first, fell in love later, got married, then had an *extremely* adorable baby girl. But, sadly, they divorced, forevermore waging text wars over what was best for their daughter. Now she splits her time between her parents' houses and is forced on vacations with *both* parents to make them *both* happy, when what she most wants is to stay home and be with friends instead of staring at cows grazing on the side of the turnpike on the way to Disney World.

Seven days in the magical land of the Mouse. Fort Wilderness, to be exact.

Seven . . . whole . . . days.

"Torture," I mumble, the word snaking around my ankles and wrists.

"You say something, Haley?" My captor's brown eyes pop into the rearview mirror.

I quickly shut mine. All I can do right now is feign sleep in the back of the van before my paternal parole officer asks any more questions. As Florida residents, we go to Disney all the time. So, why this week, of all weeks?

"Haley?"

Ignore. Earbuds are a clear sign that I'm busy.

I could be home, flitting between the DQ, beach, and Eva's and Brianna's houses. Watching Nate's butt at baseball practice until the sun goes down, finally scoring him as my summer fling. All the changes to make him see me differently, though—wasted. Last week I got red highlights in my brown hair. This week it was the purchase of the super-awesome retro yellow-and-black bikini, the nail in the coffin, so to speak. The one I was going to wear to the Fourth of July bonfire tomorrow to score my victory.

Nate would finally see the real me, not the female Jupiter Cavaliers pitcher he's been catching with for two years now, but a summer goddess to rival Katie Tillman. He would end up kissing *me*, not Katie, out on the pier. But *noooo*.

Because by the time this hookup interruptus is over, Eva and Brianna will be at Ranch Camp for the rest of the summer, and Katie will have swooped in on Nate, taking my perfectly planned prize. Thanks, Dad. And you, Erica, for thinking that I should visit you guys and that we should spend more time as a family. For pushing *Fart* Wilderness.

I am very, *very* disappointed in you both.

And you two . . .

I crack an eye open at the other prisoners, my baby twin brother and sister trying to toss tiny bits of shredded napkin at each other like they actually weigh anything, but the handmade confetti just sticks to their little fingers and car seats. They giggle, in their own world like only twins can be. I love them, but I'm outside of their inside joke. Of course I am. I'm seventeen. They're four.

"Psst." I reach out with my foot to touch their elbows.

Willy looks back at me and shows me his cute front baby teeth. "Hi, Tata."

Hi, I mouth through a smile, so my dad doesn't hear me, because I'm fake-sleeping, but Alice grabs my foot and shakes it. "Ta-taaaaaaa!"

Shhh, I mouth, finger at my lips.

My father's eyes fall on me again in the rearview mirror, eyebrows expecting a response. I pull out my earbuds. "Yes?"

"I *said* . . . are you hungry? Do you want to stop for something to eat?"

"No, I'm good." Earbuds back in.

His eyes talk to me, eyebrows moving up and down. *Ugh, now what?* I sigh and pull my earbuds out again. "Yeeess?"

"You need to eat something, Haley. You didn't eat before we left."

"I said I'm fine, Dad." Earbuds in. Resume cow watching.

For a second I glimpse Erica's eyes rolling in the side mirror. She is not a bitch by any means. She does nice stuff for me, but here's

3

the thing—it's all fake. Maybe, maybe not, but she is not the "cool big sister" she marketed herself as five years ago. And, honestly, I'm a little peeved by her false advertising.

My dad keeps driving without a word. Erica looks out her window. I know what they're thinking—they need to fix me before I turn into a wild child like my mom. But let me tell you something—I . . . do . . . not . . . need . . . fixing.

And neither does she.

One nap and two snoring toddlers later, we arrive at the mouth of the Mouse. Dad gets friendly with the Magic Kingdom parking-fee taker, letting him know that we're checking into the Fort Wilderness campground so we won't be paying at the moment. Some general pleasantries are exchanged, and I hear Dad tell the guy, "Jupiter . . . ninety minutes flat," and everybody agrees that my dad has made the best time of any father today.

"Have a magical stay!" the parking-fee taker says, and you can tell from the smile on his smooth-shaven face that he really means it.

"Yay," I murmur from the backseat, eliciting a warning eyeball from my father.

We drive in and take the right lane that heads to Disney World's only campground. Once we pass the resort's fake wood sign and security guy wearing a fake wilderness outfit that would get him beat up at my school, Dad pulls into a space and finally parks.

He reaches into the side-door recesses, fumbles with something in his lap, and slaps it on. "We're here!"

It's furry. And on his head. "Dad, the Davy Crockett hat? Really?"

He turns in his bucket seat to give me a goofy smile. "You know I wear it every year. Where's my reservation printout? Honey, have you seen it?" he asks Erica.

"Oh my God." I suppress a smile.

Fine. Disney is entertaining. My *dad* is entertaining. But I'd still rather be home with everybody else. I don't hate this place. I just resent the fact that they thought of little kids and parents, but what about us? Although . . . the *one* ride I really, truly love is the Rock 'n' Roller Coaster at Hollywood Studios. Other than that, they should add a new themed land to the Magic Kingdom, like Hot Boy Land or Leave Me Alone Town. The *cast members'* uniforms could be jeans, unlaced sneakers, and heavy eyeliner.

Erica isn't helping my dad find the papers. She's on the phone with her mother, briefing her about the trip over. "We did. . . . I did. . . . The kids are fine. They're still sleeping." She glances back to double-check Willy and Alice. Of course, *I'm* not still sleeping, but she didn't mean me.

I take advantage of the rare quiet moment and share my theme-park idea aloud with my dad. My first nongrunts since we left Jupiter. "It would be awesome to have lands like that."

"I like it, Haley." He lifts a giant plastic bag of goodies Erica packed.

"And there could be rides with restrictions for anyone under the age of fifteen," I add.

"Ooh, yes!" He changes his voice to imitate the rich baritone of a radio announcer. "This summer, come and experience the rip-roaring, plunging new double coasters, Raging Hormones and Angry Daughter.'"

My eyelids flatline. "Dad . . . stupid."

His are crinkly in the rearview mirror. "I liked it."

"Oscar." Erica lifts the phone away from her mouth. "What's so funny?" Dad stops to explain what we just talked about and his clever joke. Erica says, "Uh-huh, uh-huh," as he shares our little secret. Before you know it, she's rolling her eyes, and then it's not between just us anymore.

Sigh.

Willy and Alice wake from their drooling slumber upon hearing the excitement.

"We're here? Where's Mickey?"

"I wanna ride the train!"

I settle back into my seat again. Why couldn't Dad have kept that moment between us? It doesn't all need to be shared with Erica. He gets out of the van and slides the side door open. "I'm going to go check in. Haley, come with me."

"Why me?" I mumble.

"Just come."

Grr.

Inside the registration cabin, check-in takes forever. Or maybe it just seems that way because I'm standing next to my forty-something father, who's shamelessly wearing a coonskin hat. "We've been here three minutes, and already we're in line," I offer by way of observation.

He eyeballs me again. "Young lady, as long as you act miserable, you will be. Try to have a good time."

"Dad, one—you made me cancel my last camp session. Two—I can't even hang out with Eva and Brianna before they leave." I don't mention my plot to get with Nate. It's not like I wanted love—love is for masochists who enjoy the pain of a mangled heart. I just wanted something that would end in time for my senior year. A lot could've happened in these seven days!

We move up in line. "Haley, we don't know what the seizures are about yet. We can't have you away at camp so long when you just started the Tegretol. You can't go jumping on horses just yet."

Oh, yay. The *S* word. I was trying not to think about that. "It was *one* seizure, and the whole Internet says that only one percent of the population will ever have a second one."

"Yes, and there's only a two percent chance of getting pregnant with twins, yet *there they are!*" He gestures to the van outside containing my stepmom and mini siblings.

"But they have trained medical staff at camp. My friend Dante has epilepsy too. He stays both sessions, and they know what to do with him. Mom was perfectly fine with letting me go. Why can't you be?"

"Because . . . it's too soon," he says, ignoring my eye contact. "Now stop."

Ugh. I switch to a better use of my time—playing with my phone. I fire off a round of texts to Eva and Brianna and get sad faces back from both of them, plus pics of them hanging out together at the beach. At least the "wilderness" out here gets good reception.

I feel warm arms enveloping me. "Listen, I know this isn't what you wanted," my dad says. "I know that. But you can still try to enjoy it. I had a blast here when I was your age. You can do the same."

I wriggle out of his hug. "A 'blast'? Dad, really? Look around."

"Yes, a blast. Biking, horseback riding, canoeing, the pool. I mean, it's not the same without the Marshmallow Marsh or River Country anymore. . . ." He looks off behind the registration counter—sort of—and my eyes try to follow his line of vision. It takes him a moment to return to the present. "But it's still a ton of fun." His faraway stare melts into a sad smile.

"'A ton of fun.'" Could anything called the Marshmallow Marsh be a *ton of fun*?

"Yes, a *ton of fun*," he says in a new, annoyed tone. "Now you have a problem with the way I talk?"

"Dad, River Country closed when I was a baby, and now this place is just a bunch of trees, fake cabins, and an old arcade pizza place. We could've at least stayed at the huge Wilderness Lodge with the hot springs pool. Now *that* would've been a ton of fun."

My dad shifts his weight and moves up another inch in line. His silence suggests that I don't get it. But I do. I get that Fort Wilderness is important to *him* because it holds lots of memories. It's where he spent every summer as a kid. It's where he met my mom.

But that was a long time ago.

And a lot has happened since then.

8

Divorce and whatnot.

But can I blame him for holding on to something that no longer exists? When the possible reasons for what went wrong between my parents float around in my mind more often than I care to admit?

"Look, we did the Disney thing for you when you were a kid. Now we have to do it for Alice and Willy," Dad says.

"Really?" My eyebrows get that arc to them. I can feel something foolish coming. "Are you sure this is about Alice or Willy?"

Oof. Too snarky. A middle-aged blonde ahead of us turns around to stare at the perpetrator of such sass. Dad's laser gaze descends on me, the familiar sign that I'm crossing over into Shut Up territory. "I beg your pardon?"

He's always saying I can tell him anything, and considering this is a rare opportunity without Erica and the kids around, I clear my throat. "Dad, you have these . . . ideas . . . of us all together like some perfect TV family, when you know it's not like that. It's you, Erica, and the kids together all week, and then . . . there's *me* part of the time. You know I'm the odd man out."

That's it. That's all I'm saying.

I'm not going to complain about my life. When you compare it to the hell some other people live, it's great. But if I had to play one sympathy card, it's this: *I have to live at two houses.* Willy and Alice don't. Life would be a lot easier if my parents were still together. I know I caused some of it. I sided with Mom on most of their good-cop-bad-cop arguments about me.

According to my father, it was because Mom was "too reckless, too free-spirited." And in one particular beer-affected conversation, he actually told me there was never a love-at-first-sight factor when meeting her. *Pfft, nice, Dad.*

So where does this leave me? In the middle. Not cool, parentals. Not cool.

I can feel the tension in Dad's ten-second silence. "I don't have delusions of a TV family, honey. I was just trying to spend more time with you. That's all."

"Then, why couldn't we have spent a few days at home on the beach? Alice and Willy would've been fine with *one* day in Disney. Who's the only person who ever wants to spend a whole *week* in Fart Wilderness? You."

No eye contact from him. But plenty from others around us, including a manager type, for blaspheming about his beloved campground. "Haley, don't be selfish," Dad grumbles.

Wait. . . . Whoa. "Me? *You're* the one trying to relive your childhood memories and making *me* pay for it. How does that make me selfish?"

"Stop it now," he stage-whispers, "or you're going to understand the true meaning of pain. In five . . . four . . . three . . ."

Empty Daddy words that he's been threatening me with since I was a kid. But I'm not a kid anymore. He needs to listen to me. "I hate this place!"

A stunned hush falls over the room. *Great. Now I've done it.*

His brown eyes bear down on me, and I know I'm in trouble. But

I'm past the point of caring. He ruined my summer plans. How else am I supposed to feel?

His voice is icy. "I've heard enough, Haley. Go wait in the car."

My eyes sting. They plead with him, but they have no power anymore. Apparently, I have to be Erica for that. "Fine." I crouch under the ribbon-divider thingy in one swift movement and charge toward the main exit. Everyone in the lobby stares at me, but I don't care. It took me seventeen years to have *one* tantrum. Not bad, if you ask me.

Someone brushes by me on purpose. "Campfire by the Meadow Trading Post tonight. Nine thirty," a male voice says. When I look up, a guy and a girl about my age are exiting through the other doors. The guy, blond hair hanging in his face, looks back at me, I guess to make sure I heard him.

"It's a lame campfire," I inform him. "A sing-along and a Disney movie. And it's at seven thirty, not nine thirty."

A taller, older kid strides past me just then. "Not our campfires."

Oh. I see.

His dark brown eyes challenge me. "Nine thirty. Without your old man."

two

We drive through the campground in search of our cabin, and all I can think about is the invitation to hang out. I don't know how I'll pull off going alone under the circumstances, but I'm thinking of a plan that sometimes works with my father—entitlement.

We wind through a looped road stemming from a main middle road. All the loops look the same. They all have some fifty cookie-cutter "cabins," with loglike exteriors, fully equipped kitchens, bedrooms with one double bed and bunk beds, and a little living room with a Murphy bed that folds up into the front wall. When we finally reach our cabin, I pull down the Murphy bed and fling myself onto it.

Entitlement, Act I. "This one's mine."

My dad and Erica exchange looks. "That will be fine," Dad

says, "but don't complain when I'm out here making coffee in the morning."

"Okay." So far, so good.

We rented an electric cart for getting around the campground, so here comes *Entitlement, Act II.* "I'm also going to need the golf cart tonight when you guys are done with it."

Erica starts unpacking grocery bags full of food for our home-away-from-home kitchen. "You can't drive it without us, Haley. It's in your father's name."

"Actually, she can," Dad mumbles, dodging two screaming, car-liberated preschoolers. "I added her to the contract for emergencies. Minimum driving age is sixteen."

"Aaaahhhh!" A Willy-like blur runs by.

"I'm gonna eat you!" Alice jumps on Willy's back and tackles him to the ground.

"Really? Thanks, Dad!"

"I said *for emergencies.* I didn't say you could use it."

"What? Aw, come on."

"You can't drive yet. Are you purposefully trying to forget everything the doctor said?"

I sit up in protest. "But it's not even real driving. It's a *golf cart.*"

"Can you two argue about it while you help unload the rest of the car, please?" Erica's sighs and huffs emphasize the fact that she's unloading everything herself.

"No problem," I mutter. Helping them will show how responsible I am. I get up and follow my father outside. "Please, it's the only fun thing to do here. Nothing bad is going to happen. I'll have my phone on me the whole time."

"You barely reply to my texts, so that's not helping your argument."

"Okay, I'll reply to your *every* text. Just don't text every two minutes." I smile. "You told me to have a good time, right? Well, I would have a good time driving the cart around. You know, to explore Fort Wilderness, see what there is to see and stuff."

"We can explore as a family."

What? "No!"

He throws his hands up, then pulls me closer to the car, away from what I can only assume is Erica's range of hearing. "Haley, what is your problem? You're acting like this is all so terrible."

"It is to me."

"Really? I would disagree. You're pretty damn lucky to have two families that love you. Stop saying crap like that. Erica takes everything you say very personally. *I* take what you say personally."

I twist my arm out of his hold. "Why do you always defend Erica's feelings? What about mine?" Yes, I sound whiny, even to my ears, but this is how I feel. He needs to hear it.

He studies my eyes. He looks up and eventually sighs. "If I lend you the golf cart . . ."

Yes . . . ? I'll do anything!

"You're just going to take off, and then we'll never see you. Which is not what we're trying to accomplish here. That is the antisolution."

"It's just a GOLF CART!" I cry.

But okay . . . okay . . . I need to act more mature for this to work. I lower my voice and try to sound as rational as possible. "Dad, some kids my age are meeting after the campfire tonight. I just want to go see what they're up to. It's probably going to be boring. But I don't want to show up with Daddy and Stepmommy, you know?" My eyes plead with him. "You understand, right? Right, Daddy?"

He doesn't respond. Why is this so hard for him? I'd better start thinking of a Plan B.

I place my hands over his folded arms. "Please? Trust my judgment. I'm not going to do anything stupid. I'll be fine. Don't you trust your parenting skills enough to be comfortable with the fruits of your labor?" My eyebrows turn up for a very convincing finish.

"It's your mother's parenting skills I worry about."

"Dad. Not funny."

He smiles to himself, sighs heavily, and places his hand on the car. "Okay. But you have to answer me every time I text you. Spend the afternoon with us, then after dinner you can take it for a spin."

"Yes. Thank you." I throw my arms around him, and he leans in, enjoying the hug.

"Just try to pretend that you love us, okay?"

"What?" I take a step back and look at him hard.

His eyes don't meet mine. He starts grabbing the last of the bags from the trunk.

"Dad, it's not like that. At all. It's just . . ." He never even *asked* where I wanted to go this summer or my opinion on anything. He

15

always used to ask. When it was me, him, and Mom, he would listen to everything I said. Not anymore.

"Don't worry about it, Haley. Just come inside."

I want to say I'm sorry for acting like a brat, but a part of me really feels he deserved it. For not taking my feelings into consideration. But all I say is, "Thanks, Daddy. I love you."

He nods. "Love you too."

I go back inside, feeling victorious but sad. Can't figure out why. I just hang out, watch TV, and play with Willy and Alice as much as I can before it's time to go. I get so caught up in reruns of *The Suite Life of Zack and Cody* on the closed-circuit Disney Channel that I jump when I see it's past nine thirty p.m. "Gotta go." I grab the map and kiss the twins, their smooth little faces pressed to my pillows, a breath away from sleepy time.

"Where you going, Tata?" Alice pops up.

I gently guide her back onto the pillow. "I'm going for a ride in the—"

"She's going to the bathroom." Dad eyes me.

"Right. Bathroom." Mention a ride in the golf cart, and I'll find myself accompanied by two midgets. "So I'll see you in a bit, okay?"

"No, Tata, don't go." Alice pouts.

"Yeah, Tata, don't go," Dad says weakly, but then smiles. "Alice doesn't want you to go . . . so far . . . to the bathroom."

"Dad. Stop."

"Don't be too long," Erica adds from the adjacent kitchen. "We want to leave early tomorrow morning for Magic Kingdom, so you'll need all your energy."

"Okay."

"Have fun." Dad smiles in a sad way. "Come right back if you feel off in any way, you hear?"

"Yes, Dad." I take the cart key from the kitchen counter. "See you later." When I step into the hot night and close the door gently behind me, a deep breath fills my lungs and escapes slowly. The silence of the Florida wilderness settles around me as I slide into the golf cart.

My heart races for the first five minutes. I'm out! By myself!

Even with headlights on and the occasional streetlight, I almost miss the street I'm supposed to turn onto, it's so dark. Hard to believe that four theme parks light up the night just a couple of miles away. I recognize the pool I came to last time we were here and turn onto the electric cart road next to it. Driving around the curvy path, I hear movie music, and then slowly, a big outdoor screen appears to my left under the stars. Metal bleachers are full of families watching *Sleeping Beauty*. Nearby are two campfires surrounded by people roasting marshmallows.

I press down on the brake and pocket the key.

Stepping out, crunching over gravel, I scan the amphitheater area for the teens I saw earlier. What if they're not here? Maybe they were messing with me. If that's the case, I'll stay until the movie ends, then drive somewhere else.

"Haley," someone calls from off to one side. I look around. "Over here."

Dark figures lounge under a tree behind the concession stand. I head over, letting my eyes adjust again to the dark. As I get closer, I recognize the three kids I saw at registration.

"Hey," says the only girl. She has shoulder-length light brown hair, streaked with thick blond highlights.

"Hey. How'd you guys know my name?"

The first guy, the one who told me to meet them, breaks a twig and tosses a tiny gravel rock into the space between us. "Everyone in the lobby knew your name." He chuckles.

We were arguing that loud? Man. "Right." I put my thumbs into my jean shorts pockets. "So, what are you guys up to?"

"Plotting," says the girl, eyes focused on the phone lighting up her whole face.

"Plotting what?"

"Something to do." There's the deeper voice, the other guy who talked to me.

"Are you guys all related?" Not that it matters. Just want statuses.

"We are," the older one says, pointing at the other boy. "He's my brother. She's some crazy chick we just met." He smiles, and the girl pegs him with a piece of gravel. "Okay, she and her brother are friends of ours. We stay here for a month every summer."

"A month?" My eyebrows fly up. I can't imagine any normal family affording that. "You mean in the RVs?"

They nod. Oh, right. I forgot how many people actually live in Fort Wilderness part of the year. I guess that's cool. If you like trees.

"So where's the rest of your families?" I ask, scanning around.

"Different places. My parents are at the camper, sitting outside, having their nightly beers. Dina here"—he gestures to the girl on her phone—"is a year-rounder."

"You live here all year?" I ask her. I take a seat cross-legged across from them and start yanking at blades of grass poking through the gravel. "Why?" I laugh.

She sits back against the tree. "Not all year. I live in Kissimmee. My dad manages Pioneer Hall, the restaurants and common area over there, so I'm around a lot, like when these guys visit during the summer."

"So you're Dina," I say. "And you two are . . ."

"Jacob and Edward," the older one says, and they all start laughing. "Sorry, I meant . . . I'm Luke, and he's Han." They stifle smiles this time.

I'm pretty sure those are names from *Star Wars*. "Right, and I'm Chewbacca," I say.

We all laugh. Dina smacks them both on the arm. "They're stupid and stupider is what they are. This is Rudy and Marcus." She points out the younger, cuter one as Rudy and the older, taller one as Marcus. "They're from Michigan or something."

"Minnesota," Rudy says. He's more my age, while Marcus looks like he might've just graduated high school or even be in college. Rudy has front teeth that slightly overlap each other, but it adds character to his smile. Marcus is a good six inches taller than his brother, and his hair in his face makes his expressions hard to read. Both seem like nice guys, but I can't say I'm drawn to either one of them.

"Minnesota? Wow. So, you're forced on this trip every year?" I ask.

Rudy shrugs. "I wouldn't really say forced. It's a family tradition, since before we were born. We come each summer in three RVs, go to the parks, come back by dinnertime, grill between the campers, then chill the rest of the night. Not a bad deal."

"Better than the Smokies," Marcus adds.

"Aw, yeah, the Smokies suck," Rudy says, making a little gravel pile. "What about you?"

"Me? Oh, uh, I didn't want to come. My friends are all leaving for camp in a week. It's my dad. He made us all come, so I won't be seeing any of my friends again before school starts."

"And home is?" Marcus looks at me.

"Jupiter."

"The planet?" Rudy has a shit-eating grin on his face.

"The city in Florida." Dork. Like I've never heard that one before.

"Oh. Still cool," he says. "Anyway, we're planning something for tonight, and we need one more person. Dina's brother usually plays with us, but he's not up for it tonight."

"Why do you need one more person?" I ask.

"Scavenger hunt, so the teams can be even. What about you? You up for it?"

I'd done scavenger hunts before at Ranch Camp. My team, the Panthers, always won, because we had Sean as a secret weapon, and Sean was born to be a Navy SEAL. He could get into any building, steal anything, go anywhere without being seen. I, with a newfound penchant for passing out at unexpected moments, was probably not the best choice for this game.

"I'm not that good at scavenger hunts," I say. "There could be a dog barking right in front of my face, and I wouldn't see it."

"Perfect, you're with Dina then. Boys against girls," Marcus says, getting up.

"Hey!" Dina sneers at him. She gets up too and scoots next to me. "No offense, Haley. I know this place better than they do. But this is good. And your looks are bonus. You could get us anything we want. Go ahead, Marcus, give us the list."

Could get us anything we want? I register the look on Rudy's face and the sudden interest in Marcus's eyes. I don't really see myself as hot or anything. And it's not like Dina's not pretty too, in a classic sort of way.

I watch them interact, liking how they get along. You can tell they've known one another for a long time. You can also tell that Dina likes Rudy. Marcus may not be as cute as his brother, but he's more in charge, which makes him sort of hot. He reaches into his pocket and pulls out two folded sheets of paper. He hands Dina one. "Both teams have two hours, so at midnight we meet back here."

Whoa. What? I'm not sure I can stay out that long, but I'm not about to admit that to them. Not when they have free reign over their lives, whereas I answer to a dictator. Speaking of which, a text uncannily comes in from my dad—*Hey what's up?*

Dina looks at the list in her hand and smiles. I lean over to peer at it too as I reply to my dad with lots of exclamation marks and smiley faces, so he'll know I'm just fine. There's a long itemized list of things from around the campground, ranging from twenty points all the way up into the hundreds. "What's so funny?" I ask.

"We take turns making this list every time we play. They made it this time." She looks up at them. "I already told you guys it doesn't exist." She turns to me. "They actually think there's buried treasure on Discovery Island, out on Bay Lake, but there isn't. I've told you guys, there's a fake pirate skeleton from back when it was open to the public, but that's it. And this . . ."

She points to the number two item, marked at three hundred points—pics from the west end of River Country? "*This* is guaranteed to get you kicked out of the campground forever, so don't even think about it."

"What's so great about pics from River Country?" I ask. I mean, yes, it was Disney's first water park from when my dad was a kid, but . . . "Wait, I thought that place didn't exist anymore."

All of a sudden it's as if I've grown an extra two heads. Rudy laughs.

Marcus slaps his arm. "Dude, it's not like everyone knows. Haley, it's been closed for years, but it's still back there. Closed off to the public."

Dina points into the distance. "It's behind Pioneer Hall, right next to the lake. You can see a little bit from a boat. But these guys want west-end pics, which is from the side you can't see. Not gonna happen, guys."

"Why will it get us kicked out?" I ask.

She tilts her head at me and my apparently stupid question. "Because it's trespassing. Every fanatic that tries to break in and take pics gets arrested. They're never allowed back in, trust me." Dina's talking straight to Rudy now. This girl does not want her summer crush banned from returning to her.

"Whatever, don't get your panties in a bunch." Marcus shrugs. "I just put it there for shits and giggles."

Dina points to another item right under it. "And we also can't bring back the troll that lives in River Country, because there isn't one. You guys are morons."

Marcus's amused eyes reflect the campfire's glow. "I don't know, Dina. People say they've seen him lurking in the darkness, feeding on scraps from Pioneer Hall. I think you and other Disney folk are just protecting him because he watches over the place and you feel sorry for him."

Dina scoffs. "Yes, and the real Seven Dwarfs' house is in your loop too. It's the cute little RV with the seven mailboxes in the back."

"Ha, ha. Very funny. So the rest of the list is doable?" Rudy looks around for approval.

"Let's see. . . ." I read aloud. "A metal bucket from the Hoop-Dee-Doo Revue, a live rabbit—*a live rabbit?*" I look around at their amused faces. "A pool net from Guest Services, a saddle from the Tri-Circle-D Ranch, a swing seat from any kids' playground, and an oar. You guys really go for stolen goods." Man, my camp's scavenger hunts were all about finding stupid things, like pinecones and shells.

Marcus hands the list to his brother. "Midnight, we reconvene. Losing team buys the other team pizza for the rest of the week plus sexual favors. Ready?"

"You wish." Dina averts her eyes shyly, but I can tell she might not mind that one.

Rudy runs a hand through his hair. I don't think he even caught on to Dina's expression, because he's too busy checking me out. "So you guys use Dina's cart, and we'll use ours."

Dina opens a cinched tote bag and distributes four flashlights. Marcus helps his brother to his feet, then claps once. "Are we all ready?"

"May the best team win." Rudy smiles, then heads off toward their cart.

"That would be us," Dina says as she leads me away. "They are so going down."

"It's cool that you guys stay friends every year," I tell Dina, testing the waters.

"It is." There's a touch of sadness in her voice, but I won't pry.

We walk to a row of electric carts located behind the gravel pit I parked in. "You play this game every day?" I ask.

She shakes her head. "Nah. Maybe twice in a summer. It's become a tradition the past couple of years. You're not going to get in trouble, right? For being out late?"

"I might have to let my dad know where I am," I say, feeling like a baby for admitting that. "He's more overprotective than a hundred SPF sunblock, but I think I'll be all right."

"A hundred SPF sunblock!" Dina laughs out loud, and I smile.

I omit any talk of seizures, although technically I'm supposed to let people who are alone with me know about them and what to do in case of one. But I only had one and it was months ago, with no recurrence, so it just seems stupid to bring it up.

"Be totally sure you can stay out before we start." She unplugs a custom-painted blue electric cart from the charging station, gets in the driver's seat, and turns the key. I get in beside her and hold on as she pulls out. The hot night air suddenly surrounds us, and I revel in the freedom. "Because we're starting with the River Country pics."

I stare at her. "I thought you said you could get kicked out for trespassing."

"I said *they* could get kicked out." She steps on the gas and weaves through the Meadow Trading Post's sidewalks as only a resident would. "But I know this place inside out. My dad works here, remember? They'd slap my wrist at most. And you're with me, so I'll just take all the blame."

My dad would kill me if he knew what I was doing, but then again, he might think it's cool, since he had a *blast* there when he was little. It's hard to tell. A smile spreads across my face, the first real smile since I left Jupiter. Photos of an abandoned water park would be a kick-ass thing to brag about.

She turns onto the main road and heads for Pioneer Hall and the marina. This is where guests take boats across Bay Lake to other resorts and the Magic Kingdom. We zoom past families walking back to their cabins and others lounging around in folding chairs. Everyone's laid-back, enjoying the clear night.

I wonder how she plans on pulling this off. "Are we going to hike behind Pioneer Hall, get in through the employee entrance, jump a fence, or what?"

"You don't mind getting wet, do you?" There's a sliver—no, a whole slice—of mischievousness in her voice.

Wet? I shift my gaze from the illuminated road to Dina again. Her hair whips around her face as she drives. Her green eyes light up in the rearview mirror's reflection. Dad wanted me to have fun, right? So fun I will have. I grip my seat with both hands. "Not at all," I reply.

"Then let's do this." She smiles and steps on the gas.

three

Outside Pioneer Hall, a meeting place for Fort Wilderness guests, people stream out of the Hoop-Dee-Doo Revue, a show that's been running since before I was born. All I remember about it from when I was little is a lot of singing, actors prancing around, and metal buckets of fried chicken clanging on your dinner table. Waiting outside are horse-drawn carriages and hayrides. The area is buzzing with activity as we cut through the crowd.

We drive past the buffet restaurant and adjoining pizza place. We're near the marina, where a slew of people are retiring from the parks. Exhausted parents carry their dead-asleep kids on their shoulders, wrist-tied Mickey balloons bouncing in the air above them.

"How are we going to do this with so many people around?" I ask, eyeing a boat out on the water waiting to dock.

"We're not." Dina turns left at a playground and takes us down a dimly lit road. The farther we go, the quieter it gets, until the sloshing sounds of tied racing boats and paddleboats bobbing against the docks come into the foreground. Even in the dark, I see a near-empty beach to my right. Only a few silhouettes sit there, heads touching. "We have to wait till everyone leaves."

"And you're sure this is a good idea?" I mean, it's quieter around here, but I still see people, and that means people can see us.

"You don't have to if you don't want to." She slows down, then stops altogether.

At first I wonder what the heck we're doing here stopped. But then I look straight ahead, and my heartbeat suddenly sinks to my stomach. There, looming in the shadows, is a tall, brown, iron fortress of a wall stretching all the way to the beach on one side and disappearing behind Pioneer Hall on the other. A sign on it shows Goofy in an old-fashioned striped swimming suit:

RIVER COUNTRY

CLOSED PERMANENTLY

"We're here." Dina takes a moment to check her texts. She's probably used to a sight like this, but I've never laid eyes on this wall before and can't tear them away. Something about it, blocking the view of something vast and abandoned on the other side makes me feel really, *really* sad.

"When exactly did this place close?" I ask.

"Like 2001, I think," she mumbles.

Whoa. It's surreal that the water park my mom and dad were always talking about is still here, just sitting in the darkness for this long. I've never been here, not even as a baby.

I slide out of the cart to get a better look. The gate is rusted around the edges, like it was meant to be there temporarily but ended up staying much longer. For a second I think I hear people laughing and shrieking on the other side, but the sounds are coming from the crowds way behind me, maybe echoing off the wall.

Dina mumbles something about her phone, but I can't focus on her. It's awful how this sidewalk ends right here. Like, boom, dead end. But you just know it continues on the other side of that wall. Where would it take me if the barrier weren't there? Once upon a time, my parents walked down this same sidewalk when they were kids, yet I never will. I imagine my dad holding Ampa's hand, skipping all the way to the park's ticket booth. My heart aches. The vision fades, and the iron construction wall stares down at me again.

"Did you hear me?"

I turn around. "Huh?"

"I said, creepy, isn't it?" Dina nods at the wall.

"Oh. Yeah." I know this sounds crazy, but I think it's more beautiful than creepy. Finding a place that no one else cares about anymore. It feels exclusively mine, this little corner of the campground. I want to hide here all seven days.

"Haley, get in. We have to wait on the beach for a bit," Dina says.

Slowly, I tear my gaze away from the fortress and get back into the cart.

She does a quick one-eighty and heads back the way we came, but we don't go far. She turns left down a short sidewalk leading to the dark beach. I can still see the wall from here, retreating into the shadows. Stopping completely, she pops up. "Get up a sec?" I slide out, and Dina lifts the seat cushion we were sitting on. Inside is a storage compartment with some bungee cords. She rummages to the bottom and pulls out a small Ziploc bag. "Crap. There's only one. I'm going to have to go get another."

"For what?"

"Our phones go in one so they don't get wet, but we still need another one for the flashlights. I'm going to run to Pioneer Hall a minute and grab a bigger one. You wait here and keep an eye out for the boys, okay?"

"Okay. So I guess you were really serious about getting wet." I laugh nervously.

"Well, swimming along the lake's edge is the only way to get in without staff seeing us."

"What should I do if I see the guys?"

"Just text me." She grabs my phone, enters her number, and calls herself for a second. "I shouldn't be gone more than two minutes." I watch her run off, and then I'm alone with the softly lapping waves, the iron wall, and the smooching couple down on the sand.

I sit back in the golf cart and prop my feet up. Looking out at Bay Lake, I have to admit, this place is really nice. Ranch Camp has a lake, but it doesn't have soft sand like this, pretty lit-up boats traveling back and forth, or an awesome view of the famous Contemporary Resort across the water like this one does. All staging aside, Disney World is situated on some super-pretty real estate.

Sitting here, I feel my stomach start to tighten. In just a few minutes we're going to break into the famously forgotten River Country. I glance over at the wall. Still there. Still solid. What a waste behind it. A water park just sitting there empty. I place my iPhone into the plastic bag and zip it up.

Through the plastic, I check the time—it's been one minute since Dina ran off—and stick it back in my pocket. No sign of the boys. Twenty minutes since we split up. I wonder what items they've gotten so far. How are they going to pry a swing off a swing set?

Craziness.

My thoughts are interrupted by laughter again. Not people down on the beach laughing, but faraway laughing. And water splashing, like it's coming from the lake itself. Who the hell would be in it at this time? Yes, I know *we're* about to be in the lake, but it's still weird that someone else would have the same idea as us at the exact same time.

I have to see who's making that sound. My sandals fling sand as I trudge down the beach. The romantic couple gets up to leave, oblivious to my presence. I stand on the very edge of the property and listen. Water splashes against the docks; a boat horn goes off far away. I can see the glow from the Magic Kingdom in the sky to the northwest. This is weird. I know I heard laughter. I walk over to the tall iron wall and press against it. Closing my eyes, I try to block out all other sounds.

A mosquito buzzes near my ear. I shoo it away and just stand there, smooth cold metal against my hand. Then a sense of déjà vu comes over me, standing here on the edge of the lake, hearing laughing, splashing sounds, and the pops and whistles of fireworks overhead. I hate déjà vu. I can never remember where I've seen something before, and that totally bothers me. But it doesn't this time. Instead, it's like I know this place. But that's crazy. I've never, ever been to this side of Fort Wilderness. Not only that, but when I open my eyes . . .

There're no fireworks.

I stare out at the dark edges of the water, the shrubs and foliage lurking there, and I can almost imagine the rest of the lake's edge behind this wall. I'm staring so hard, I think I'm going to lose my balance. My heart beats so strong, I can hear it in the stillness. I have to wait for Dina. She's my ticket out in case we get caught.

But my mind and body won't listen to reason at the moment.

I don't know how or why—I really can't explain it—but before I can think, rationalize, or anything, I slip out of my sandals and throw myself waist deep into the lake. I have to see it. Whether anyone spots me or not doesn't matter, because I have to get inside—now. I know this place. I push through the water, feeling the slimy bottom, the waving grasses, and God knows what else. I wade toward trees that live in the water—cypresses, I think—and feel the bottom dropping out underneath me, the black waters of the lake rising up to my chin.

What the hell am I doing? Why am I doing this? All it takes is for one person on one of those shuttle boats out there to see me, and it's all over.

I swim quickly in the cool lake, following the curve of the land until the noises grow louder. But it could be me, I remind myself. Sounds travel. People could be laughing anywhere around this lake, and I would hear it. Ahead of me, there's brush and tall grass and some old wooden boardwalk. *The nature trail.* I've been here; I've seen this.

"Haley!" Someone calls me.

I swim faster. *Get to the boardwalk.* The darkness of the lake and the buzzing of a thousand swamp insects remind me that this isn't Disney World right now. These are Florida swamps, and they were here first. My soaked shirt and shorts weigh me down. As I swim, a part of me feels like I'm not actually here. Like I fell into some strange dream where I have no control and I'm being pulled in deeper. Any minute now I'm going to wake up in a cold sweat and find that I'm in our cabin, surrounded by my sleeping family.

There could be snakes in these waters. There could be alligators. There could even be trolls, according to Marcus. The wooden board-walk is within my reach. Two more strokes.

"Haley!" Louder and clearer this time, but still far away. I think it's Dina, but I can't answer. I can hardly breathe. I reach the nature trail boardwalk and grab on to it. *Got it.* I hoist myself up, but the wooden beam snaps in my hand. It's rotting. In fact, now I can see that most of the bridge is torn down. *Swim alongside it. You'll reach the edge of the marsh, then you can walk through the trees.* I don't know how I know this, but I follow my instincts.

"Haleeeey! Where are you?"

Little by little, I feel the bottom of the lake again with my bare toes. I grab a bunch of tall grasses to pull myself closer to the shore. Something moves past me in the water. A fish or turtle, I hope. The water level drops to my knees as I stand and grab hold of tree roots, branches, and I don't know what else, because I can't see a damned thing.

Dripping wet, standing against the tree, I catch my breath. The air smells of wet grass, rotting wood, and a mustiness I can't quite name. Between gulps of air, I laugh to myself. When did I become a criminal? Part of me wants to cheer over what I just did, but another grasps the stupidity of it. What if I don't make it out as easily? What if there's security in here? How do I explain to the Wilderness Police that I couldn't control what just happened, that it was like River Country was calling me, and I had no choice but to swim toward it? If they don't arrest me on the spot, then they'll stick me in a mental institution.

So. I'm here; now what? I stand there and take it all in.

Crickets chirp all around me in the darkness, and after a minute my eyes adjust. Everywhere I look, there's tall grass, vines, and trees. Deep breath, Haley. Start walking. Slowly. I should probably have my phone ready to take pictures. I fumble inside my pocket and unlock the plastic bag to get it ready. My phone has about ten

texts from Dina and another two from my dad—*where r u? hello?*
With wet, shaky fingers, I reply—*sitting on the beach watching fireworks.
Be there soon.*

As I'm sending off the text, another one comes in from Dina,
about seeing my sandals and knowing I went in without her, and
she's coming after me. Do I answer? I will in a minute. For now
I just like the solitude of having this place entirely to myself. But
I know it's not a smart idea, considering my medical history, so I
start replying to her.

But then, somewhere to my left, twigs snap, as if they're getting
stepped on.

Crap.

Forget this. I have to get out of here. I place my phone back in the
bag, but I can't swim back again. That took every ounce of stamina
I had, and it's made me a little dizzy. I know that all Disney resorts
have behind-the-scenes connecting service roads. There has to be
one around here somewhere. I'll find it, then get the hell out. If
someone finds me, I'll just say I got lost.

At least that's my plan.

Finally, I'm out of the thicket of trees, and the stars hover over me
once again. I'm in a wide-open area. The ground I tread is covered
in tall grass and a layer of mucky water. For every sloshy footstep, I
think I hear another one behind me. It can't be Dina. She couldn't
have swum here that fast. So that leaves a Disney employee, a rac-
coon, or a swamp troll. I speed up and use my phone's screen to
illuminate where I'm going.

Darkness, more darkness . . .

My breath is loud in my ears. I feel like I know where I'm going, though I'm pretty certain I've never been here. In fact, I'm not even surprised when I stop suddenly, because out of the gloom appears a collection of shapes, hard to discern, and I slow down to take it all in. Man-made structures come into focus—wooden platforms and tall poles just sitting there frozen in a foot of swamp water. A dock for jumping off of and two suspension bridges for delving farther into the murkiness on either side of my view. I hear shrieking again in my mind. And this time I see someone grabbing a metal bar and swinging off the platform, whooping and hollering as he flings himself into the green water.

But when I blink again, there's nobody. And no water. Just an empty, slimy lake bed to my left and shallow marsh topped with a layer of algae in front of me. In another spot, two kiddie slides, embedded in big, reddish boulders, slope down and plunge into a patch of marsh grasses. Holy crap, that used to have water and kids playing in it. In fact, this whole abandoned corner of the world I am standing in now used to have hundreds of people swimming, laughing, and having a good time.

I can't believe it. I can't believe I'm seeing this.

River Country.

This is . . . there're no words for this. I swallow stagnant air and blink back the sadness rising in my throat. I hear country banjo music coming from somewhere.

Something white, winged, and startled by my presence rises into the air and disappears into the branches of a nearby cypress tree. Slowly, other structures come into view. Intertwined waterslides twist out and then retreat back into the great masses of brush, like ghostly snakes struggling to break free from the vines restraining them. Behind them are giant mounds of rock, and off to my left, other slides and ruins that might have once served a purpose. Now they sit rotting, completely forgotten by time.

Snap.

Another twig breaks somewhere in the trees, but I will *not* stick around to find out why. I take off running toward the bridge to my right, the one that flanks the lake. My feet disturb the still water, upsetting the slime layer that probably hasn't moved in years, making splashes that sound loud even to me. I jump onto the suspension bridge and run over the wooden planks, shaking and creaking the whole thing as I go. When was the last time someone walked on this thing? The ropes holding it up seem surprised at being tense again.

It's hot. Really hot. My dizziness returns. The sheer stupidity of going somewhere remote alone just four months after I had my first seizure slaps me hard; I honestly don't know what came over me. I can't think about it right now. I just need a place to hide. Luckily, I don't hear anyone behind me anymore, but I run to the end of the bridge anyway.

When I get to the end, I jump off, landing at the base of the rock mountain where the snakelike waterslides come out. My bare feet burn from running. A wooden sign lies on the ground.

WELCOME TO WHOOP 'N' HOLLER HOLLOW. FOR YOUR ENJOYMENT, PLEASE . . . STRONG SWIMMERS ONLY. Somewhere, there has to be a set of steps leading up to the top of those rocks. From there I can probably find a service exit, water-pump shed, or some cavern to duck into while I text Dina.

"Haley!" she faintly calls from the general direction I broke in through.

"Dina!" I call back this time, my voice sounding loud in my ears and strangely out of place. Apparently, I'm not loud enough, because she doesn't answer me. And then the dream feeling is back, the disconnected, slow-motion wooziness that makes me feel as though I'm out of my own body, as though I'm watching this all unfold from behind a sheet of glass.

Carefully, I climb a set of steps carved into the rock structure all the way to the top, and just when I think I've outmaneuvered whatever it was, I hear feet again, shuffling down below. My stomach crunches into a ball. Now what? Quickly, I scan around for a place to hide, but it's even darker up here surrounded by more trees and brush. I turn, nearly slamming into a giant wagon wheel covered in vines. Suddenly I'm smacked with the feeling of air displacement. There's another presence just a few feet away. My body freezes. I don't breathe. In the shadows, whatever is there is waiting for me to make a move.

My damn phone starts ringing in my pocket. I can't silence it. All I can do is stand there, poised to pounce, listening.

"Haley!" Dina's voice sounds farther away than before.

I'm here, I say in my head.

Feeling a presence near me, having nowhere to hide, and breathing the heavy heat and humidity swimming around my head, I start losing focus. I close my eyes to steady myself. My heart pounds loudly but feels uneven in my tight chest. I can't speak . . . can't respond to Dina . . . can't . . .

Oh, God.

A familiar gripping sensation overtakes me, and suddenly everything begins to swirl. *Oh, no, no.* I grab something—wood or rock, I don't know—to keep from falling. The trees seem to tilt, but it's not the trees. It's me, swaying, falling, body hitting something hard and blunt, cracking branches underneath me. Slow-motion dream and dark sky. Stars swirl above like a spinning light show, until I can't see them anymore.

Don't know where I am.

Tumbling, sliding, plunging down . . .

Tunnel.

Plummet . . . flail . . . into purple darkness.

Brace.

Hit. And then . . .

Billowy, underwater silence.

four

"Miss? Miss, are you okay?"

I cough water. My tongue hurts.

"I think she's waking up."

"Don't crowd her. Give her room."

All around me I hear water rushing, kids screeching, and people talking in hushed tones. Except for this one guy who sounds like he's in charge. "She's coming to."

My eyes hurt. My head hurts. I'm outdoors. I know the sun is out because I see orangey red behind my eyelids. I'm lying on sand, I think.

"Miss, can you hear me? Are your parents here?"

I can hear you. My parents wouldn't be here together.

"Just give her a minute."

A different voice, a woman's. "Did she slide with you? How come you didn't see her, Becky, for goodness' sake!"

"Mommy, she was already there when I slid down the slide," a little girl cries. "I fell right on top of her!"

"Ma'am"—the guy in charge is talking again—"she couldn't have slid with her. The lifeguard up there makes each person wait until the person ahead of them passes the orange flag. Then they can slide." I crack my eyelids open to peek at him. "My guess is she fainted when she entered the water." He's crouched on his knees hovering over me, but he's talking to people around him. He has black hair and a white tank top. And a mustache. Like, an actual mustache.

"It might've been a seizure." Another guy's voice, somewhere behind my head.

"But she wasn't on the slide, I'm telling you!" the little girl continues to argue with her mother. Her blond pigtails are dripping wet, and she has a pink one-piece on. "She wasn't ahead of me in line!"

"Ow. My tongue hurts." I bit it.

The people around me—I see them now, there're like ten or more of them—are all watching me, though it's hard to see their faces with the sun shining directly above them. "She's opening her eyes. She's talking."

"Told you it was a seizure," that guy says again. This makes the tank top guy in charge come closer, taking up my whole view. He looks like a lifeguard.

41

"Miss, don't move. You passed out in the water. Now you're on the beach. Just tell me your name so I can find your folks."

"I found you in the water," the blond girl says, crouching close to my face, "or else you might've *died*."

Thank you, I say, or think I say. I don't even know where I am. What is this place? Where's Mom? Or am I with Dad today? Is this camp? I can't even think of my name. I can't talk. I have to get up. "Ow."

"You sure you want to do that?" A whistle around his neck dangles above my face. He turns his attention back to the people standing around us. "It's common following a seizure for the victim to be confused." He turns to me. "Are you confused?"

Right now, I'm more irritated by his questions than anything. I want a place to lie down that's not in front of a bunch of people in weird bathing suits. I sit up, trying to get onto my feet. The crowd makes room for me. The upside-down lifeguard offers his hand. "Here, let me help you."

I look at this tanned hand a moment, then take it. He pulls me easily to my feet. He's wearing shorts that are a little on the short side. The lifeguard steadies me, then lifts a walkie-talkie to his mouth. "This is Jake at RC. We need a medic unit, pronto. Over." He attaches it to his waistband and holds my arms as a reply crackles through the speakers. Jake says, "You need me to carry you?"

"Uh, I'm fine. This happens all the time. Thanks," I say. Actually, I don't remember this happening ever. I think. Or has it? Yes, once before. In school, right before my exams.

The mustached lifeguard, Jake, taps the younger guy, the one who said I told you so, on the shoulder. "Jason, walk her to a picnic table. See if you can find her folks, and keep an eye out for the medics. I gotta get back to my post, man."

"Sure thing. Come on." Jason nods, placing his hand softly against my back. He's tall, tanned, and wearing a thin gold chain around his neck, and the hairs on his arm shine yellow in the blazing sunlight. Why I notice this above everything else, I do not know. "What's your name?"

"Haley," I say, but for a second I'm not sure. Is it? Yeah, that sounds right. Haley . . . Haley . . . "Petersen." I start heading across the sand. It's a weird beach. There's no ocean. Just a lagoon-type thing. Not sure where I'm going. And why don't I see anyone I know? I look at my guide again. "I take it you're Jason."

"Yup, but this isn't Camp Crystal Lake, so you don't need to worry." He laughs softly. I have no idea what he means by that. He must see my blank expression. "Uh, never mind. That was stupid, what I just said. Not everybody's seen that movie." He shakes his head, chastising himself.

"It wasn't stupid. I just . . . I'm not . . . ," I mumble. Is he talking about *Friday the 13th*? That's kind of a random thing to tell someone.

"Like I said, never mind."

I shield my eyes from the sun to scan the beach. Are my parents here? Which one am I with today? Where the hell am I, and why are so many people wearing the same tacky shorts? They're like running shorts with a white border along the hem and side.

"It's all right. You're disoriented. That's why I shouldn't be joking with you. So, Haley, any idea where your folks are?"

Folks. They really like that word around here.

I stop dead on the beach and really search for someone I know. Anyone. I don't remember coming here, but I couldn't have come alone, could I? I see green sun umbrellas, tan beach chairs, the old kinds, with plastic straps across the frames, and a lot of kids of all ages standing on a wooden bridge over the water, but no one I recognize. "That water's really green," I say.

"It's from the lake. It's got bromine in it. You haven't the faintest idea where your parents are, do you?" He puts his hands on his hips and peers at me, his eyes squinching in the sun so that I can't tell what color they are. Even *he's* wearing the same weird shorts. High on the waist. It doesn't stop him from being cute, though, in a blond, retro-fresh, all-American way.

"Where'd you get those shorts?" I'm sure they must be a uniform. He's probably embarrassed to be wearing them. I force a smile to show him I'm just teasing.

He looks down at them. "JByrons, I think. What's wrong with them?"

"J-what?"

His eyebrows crunch together. He examines me from head to toe. "Well, I suppose a girl who dresses like a shipwreck castaway wouldn't shop there, huh?"

Shipwreck? I look down. I'm wearing the most normal tight white tank and jean shorts ever, artfully ripped at the hem, a little drippy at the moment, maybe, but he talks like he's never seen clothes before. It would be good if I could find someone a little less clueless to help me.

"Let's go wait for the medics over there," he says.

"No. Listen, Jason, I appreciate your help, but I got it all under control. Seriously, this happens all the time." It doesn't, but the last thing I need is medical attention when I don't even know where I am, and I feel fine now. I'll just call my mom; everything will be fine. Instinctively, I feel my pocket for my phone.

"I insist, Haley. Come on. They'll just check you out a minute, and you'll be on your way."

There it is. I pull out a plastic bag, and—*why* is my phone in a plastic bag? "Sorry, I'm just going to call my—" I freeze, staring at my baggied phone. Now I remember. Dina—a girl named Dina told me to put it in a bag so it wouldn't get wet. We were going to swim. We were doing a scavenger—

Jason comes up to me and stares at my phone. "What in the world?"

"I know, I don't usually keep it in a Ziploc, but it's just that . . ."

He picks up the bag by the corner and examines it like it's dog poo. "What *is* this?"

"What does it look like?" Okay, now this is just silly. It's like I've landed on a different planet. He's never seen an iPhone? Oh, wait, he means he's never seen this model. "I know, it's the old iPhone. I was going to trade it in for the new one, but my dad's about to switch contracts, and, anyway, I want the new iPad for my birthday."

Jason hands me back the plastic bag. "Sure, whatever you say." He stares at me like I just fell out of the sky, like I'm the strange one, even though that girl standing there staring at me is wearing a headband and a rainbow one-piece bathing suit when she obviously has the body to be rocking a bikini.

God, I have *got* to find my way out of here.

"Hey, are you all right?" Jason asks.

"Yeah." *No.*

I've seen that bridge before. In fact, I've seen those waterslides, except they weren't so clean. They didn't have water gushing out, and they didn't have people on them. I have to sit down, gather my bearings, and call someone. I march all the way across the sand toward the tree-lined shore where there're fewer people. This place is really packed.

Bah. I have no signal here.

I plop down and try to think, even though Jason, following me, has made it difficult. He sits next to me and draws in his knees. "You sure? Because you still seem a bit off-kilter. I don't feel right leaving you alone. I'm sorry. I know that's the chauvinist pig in me talkin', but I don't."

"A what pig?" I ask, but then a familiar sight out across the water, behind a spattering of little blue and red boats, distracts me. I'd know that A-shape building anywhere. "The Contemporary," I mutter, my eyes fixed on the famous hotel. Wait, I'm in Disney! I came here with my dad and Erica. I have a little brother and sister. We're staying in Fort Wilderness!

I look down at my phone again. There's an unread message—*r u inside river country? i'm here looking for u.*

"River Country . . . yes," I mumble.

I turn and take another good look around.

White sandy beach, people in old-looking bathing suits, Bay Lake, inner tubes, and those wooden beams and wire? Kids sliding down a zipline, holding on to a metal handle. They hit the other end of a wood pole and fall into the water. Behind that are the waterslides, and these people on the bridge? They're in line for the slides. The line starts at those big rocks over there. I remember those big rocks, but it wasn't like this when I last saw it.

"Yup. River Country," Jason says, scooping up a handful of sand and letting it out slowly. "The ol' swimmin' hole."

I press the center button on my phone to return to the main screen, but I hold it a tad too long and Siri's bloop sound pops up.

"Did that thing just make a noise?" He leans in to study my phone. "It looks like a personal video game machine. Can I see?"

"But . . ." I tear my eyes away from all the people and really look at Jason for the first time. Blue. His smiling eyes are blue. How is this possible? "But River Country is closed," I say cautiously. Of course it is. I saw it empty and abandoned. That lake area was over-grown swamp, and that pool and kiddie area were drained and full of grass. I saw it!

"Closed?" Jason glances at his black plastic watch. He presses a silver button until it beeps. "Nah, it's Thursday." He smiles at me. "Today we're open till seven."

five

Jason seems wholesome and pure. And a little clueless, apparently. Not the kind of guy who would play a joke on anyone, especially a girl he just met, a girl who just awoke from a seizure. "Please tell me you're kidding."

"Why would I be? We really do close later on Saturdays." He shakes his head. He didn't understand that I meant closed *permanently.* "Do you have somewhere you need to be? You lost track of time or something?"

I take my wet hair and twist it nervously. "Are you sure this place isn't closed to the public? Like, open only for private parties? Because I was told . . ." I pause, then let out a heavy sigh. What I was told makes no sense right now.

His mouth is slightly parted, and he seems to be trying to

understand this strange language called English that I'm speaking. "Miss, I don't know what you're talking about. First, let me find your parents or where you're supposed to be staying." He stands up and brushes the sand off his legs. "What loop are you in?"

"Twenty-one hundred." I remember that from when my dad was driving around, trying to find our cabin.

Again, he shakes his head, then looks at me, disappointed. "Our loops aren't numbered. Little Bear Path, Bobcat Bend . . . any of those sound familiar?"

"No. Not at all."

"Why don't you come with me, and I'll let you use the courtesy phone to call your trailer. You just press star nine then your trailer number."

"I'm not staying in a trailer. I'm staying in a cabin. It's twenty-one hundred loop. I remember it clearly."

"Miss . . ." He stands there with his hands on his hips. "I don't know what it is, but it's like you just got left behind along with E.T. We don't have cabins in Fort Wilderness. I think you got your campgrounds crossed. Let me guess, you don't know what *E.T.* is either."

"Of course I know what *E.T.* is!" I place my hands at my hips to appear more sure of myself. "My dad only made me watch the twentieth-anniversary edition like fifty times when I was little."

He smirks. "The movie *I'm* talking about just came out last month. Steven Spielberg?" He shrugs, walking away from me in a hurry.

I scramble to my feet and start following him. He may be cute, but he can't tell me that *E.T.* came out last month. I know when *E.T.* came out, and it wasn't June, wasn't this year, and definitely wasn't while I've been alive. It was a long-ass time ago, so he'd just better lose the attitude, or else I'm going to have to . . .

Wait a minute. He's really leaving. "Jason, hold up!"

There's a family just arriving and settling into the picnic table that was next to us a moment ago. The father's hair is layered, and he wears a beige suit that looks like it's made from terry cloth. The older boy has white socks all the way to his knees. Hot! And the younger boy has on these big headphones wired to a small yellow box in his hand. Is that . . . ?

"Hey, man, neat Walkman. Is that waterproof?" Jason asks, passing him by.

"Thanks. Yeah, it is. I just got it today!" The boy smiles at him, then at his dad, and then the whole family looks at me funny as I try to keep up with Jason.

"Jason, hold on. Wait. Can you wait, please?"

He stops, puts his hands on his hips, and sighs. "What is it? Look, first you make fun of my dolphin shorts when yours look like a shipwreck. Then you try telling me that there're cabins when I've known this place for eleven years, and what we have are *trailers*. You won't tell me what that device is you got there, and now you're questioning my knowledge of new movies?" He huffs. "I just used up my entire break trying to help you. You're free to use the courtesy phone. The medics should be here any moment. But I need to get back to work."

"Just . . . Can you just answer one question for me, please? One question, and then I'll leave you alone. I promise." He keeps walking, and I have to run ahead of him, then turn around to get him to stop. My feet start burning on the hot sidewalk. "Where do you work?"

"Towel rental booth. Your one question is up."

"No. No, no, no, that wasn't it. Okay, look, please don't think I'm crazy—"

"Too late." He crosses his arms. I'm trying really, really hard not to notice his tanned biceps when he does that. I don't remember any Disney cast members being this friggin' cute any other time I've stayed here.

I point at him. "That's . . . that's very funny. And entirely understandable." I take a step closer to him. I honestly don't want anyone overhearing what I'm about to ask. He seems taken aback by my closing in on him. "Okay, here goes. Ready?" I let the words float out of my mouth as sensibly as possible. "What . . . year is it?"

He gets that look again, where he's trying to understand my language, read my face, my thoughts, analyzing everything. He's killing me here with this nonresponse thing of his. Then what does he do? He laughs. "Whoa, that is just radical, man. I can't believe I fell for that." He brushes past me.

"What? I'm serious. That's my question for real, Jason. *What year is it?*"

He turns around, and it's as if he suddenly remembers his Disney cast member manners. "Miss, it's July first, 1982." He smiles a big Disney smile. "Is there anything else I can do for you today?"

A lightning bolt shoots out of the sky and splits me in two as I stand there looking at him. At least it feels that way. Nineteen eighty-two? As in 19 . . . 82?

As in my mom and dad were . . . fifteen and sixteen?

Slowly, a smile spreads across my face. I laugh. This is great. This is just friggin' fantastic! I'm just going to enjoy this until I wake up, and then I'm going to write it all down as the awesomest, most vivid, wacky-packy dream I have ever had in my entire life. "No, that's all, thank you."

"You're very welcome. Have a magical stay here in Walt Disney World!" Jason smiles politely, then proceeds to make his way behind the help counter at the rental shop.

"Thank you!" I call out, watching him assist the next customer, a mom with a striped shirt tucked into white, elastic-banded shorts, and her little girl with pleated barrettes in her hair, carrying a Strawberry Shortcake doll. The girl has on light blue shoes that look like they're made of jelly, and I *so* want a pair!

I love this dream!

But there's only one way to know if it really is or not. I turn back around, open up my camera app, and start snapping off picture after picture of the famous River Country. The green lagoon ahead of me; the quiet beach area to my right, next to all the cypresses I swam through; and the blue pool to my left, where people are plunging down two slides that drop them about six feet above the water level.

Those had vines all over them just yesterday, or whenever it was that I last saw them. If it's all still on my phone when I wake up, then I wasn't dreaming.

I smile and take in the sights and sounds. Even the smells of suntan lotion and BBQ cooking from somewhere nearby. I can't send these photos until I have a signal, but at least I have them. And just to ensure that Dina, Rudy, and Marcus don't think I stole these off the Internet, I turn around and snap off a few selfies with the water park in the background as well.

Say River Country!

"I see you're feeling better," someone says. Shielding my eyes, I find the source of the voice lying on a long towel on a lounge chair in a really cute red bikini. "I was over there when they pulled you out of the water. It was a bit scary, I gotta say. Glad you're okay, though."

She sort of looks like Dina in that sandy-blond-hair way, but a tad older and with feathered hair. She opens a little door in her music player, flips a cassette tape around, closes it, and presses down the play button. Then she puts big foamy headphones over her ears and closes her eyes against the sun. I take a quick pic of her, too.

I sit in the grass bordering the sandy tanning area. *Think, Haley. What do you do?* A good plan would be to Google symptoms of seizures again. Back when I had my first one in March, I read somewhere that people sometimes experience time-travel hallucinations during one. This could be one. Yet it's all so real. These chairs, that loglike garbage can right over there, that water tower that says RIVER COUNTRY, the people having a good time. How can any of this be a dream? But I can't research anything, because according to Jason, it's 1982, so there're no computers, that I know of, much less Google.

Next plan . . .

I watch Jason inside the rental booth. Look at him. He's already forgotten about me as he hands out tickets and towels. Given a different haircut and a better pair of shorts, that dude would make the perfect summer fling in real time. He's sweet, even though I exasperated the heck out of him. But there's no point in flinging with him, because I have to find my way out of this hallucinogenic episode of *Doctor Who.*

But how do I do that? Find my way back home?

Jason catches me staring at him. Embarrassed, I look away. A moment later my gaze finds its way to him again. He's writing something on a clipboard. He turns it around, and I'm a little surprised when I see that it's for me. In permanent marker, he wrote: "Medics on their way. Wait there." Is that how they did it before texting? How cute!

I nod, but the thing is, I can't wait for the medics. How will I explain where I came from?

"He's a bit the loner type, but cute," Red Bikini Girl says. She taps her feet to the music. "I'm partial to Jake, his older brother, but Jason's nineteen. Perfect for you."

"Oh, I don't really . . ." *Whoa. Nineteen? Nice.*

"Honey, girls have been swooning left and right since he started working here last month, yet he hasn't dated a single one of them. You've gotten the most attention out of any girl here. That makes you the pick of the litter."

What makes her think he'd want to date me? He can hardly stand me!

A second later a guy appears next to us, oiled and shiny, brandishing two big cups of soda—one for her, one for himself. He looks a little young for her, judging from his skinny body type, if I could only get a look at his face.

She looks up, surprised, and takes the drinks. "Oh, thanks, Oscar. You didn't have to do that."

Oscar? Funny, that's my dad's name.

"This is my friend, uh . . ." Bikini Girl waits for me to give her my name.

"Haley."

"Oscar, this is Haley."

The guy sits on the lounge chair next to her, and . . . no . . . way. I see the familiar, sunny-eyed smile I've known all my life, minus thirty pounds, the gray hair, and, apparently, the ability to recognize me. You have *got* to be kidding me!

Deep breaths, Haley.

Dad? Paternal parental? *No way! No friggin' way!*

Immediately, I feel like he's going to yell at me for not answering his texts. My instinct is to turn around and run. But then I remember—1982. My dad has never even seen me before! He can't possibly know who I am.

"Hey, Haley. Nice to meet you." As soon as I hear his voice, his identity is confirmed. *Oh my God, Dad!* He smiles a smile I adore, have always adored, and does a little *what's up* nod.

Someone taps my shoulder lightly. "Miss, are you the one needing medical attention?" Which is great, because staring at my dad as a teen right here in front of me, I just about have another seizure.

six

I look at the Disney paramedic with his white shorts, white shirt, and first aid kit. "Yeah, give me just a minute, will ya?" I turn back to my dad and wave cautiously. "Hi there."

He looks at me oddly. I can't say I blame him. I'm a stranger who should be going off with the paramedic instead of lingering around staring at him.

Apparently, Bikini Girl feels the need to explain. "Haley was feeling a bit sick over there at the lagoon, but Jake and Jason pulled her out." She takes a sip of her drink.

"Oh, I get it." My dad nods politely, but with a look that suggests I need to get a move on. One, because there's a paramedic waiting patiently for me, and two, because I'm probably messing up his game with hot, older chick here. "You're still looking a little pale, though.

Maybe you should get a drink too. You want me to get you one?"

"That's very nice of you, but I'm good. I was on my way out anyway. Thanks." I turn to the paramedic. "I'll be fine. I don't really need—"

"You know, you look a lot like my cousin," my dad tells me suddenly, squinting up at me. "Where are you from?"

I can't tell him Jupiter. My family has lived in Jupiter all our lives. It would raise a red flag. "Uh . . . Atlanta." It's the first thing that falls out of my mouth. If Dad is here, Anma and Ampa must be here too.

"Where in Atlanta?" And even though, technically, I'm a year older than him, I feel obligated to answer his interrogation. But this is enough. I've absorbed too much for one half hour. I need to get away for a bit and rest my brain. Plus I need shoes.

"Peachtree Street." Or something. "Well . . . great to meet you . . . *Oscar* . . ." I back away slowly. I just called my dad Oscar. "And, uh, I'm not sure I got your name," I say, looking at Bikini Girl.

"Marsha."

"Marsha, Oscar . . ." I back into a trash can, making a super-loud crashing sound, and they look at each other, trying to suppress their laughs. I need to exit . . . now. "I'll see you guys later?"

"For sure. We're always around. Just look for us here or on the beach."

"I will do that!" I'm practically yelling.

Wow . . . wow! My dad! In 1982? Right where he said he always spent all his summers! And he was getting his game on with a girl who seemed older than me! How unfatherly, not to mention awkward. Quickly, I turn around and realize I forgot all about the dude in the white shorts and white shirt waiting for me. "Ready? Right this way, ma'am."

Breathe, breathe, Haley.

If my dad is here, could my mom be too? They met in Fort Wilderness, and supposedly Mom's family and Dad's family would stay in the same loop every year. I don't know what to make of all this. I'm pretty sure I'm going to wake up any moment, and everything will be back to normal. Except I will never be normal after this.

"Where are we going?" I ask the paramedic, stopping for a moment to slip on a pair of brown flip-flops belonging to someone else who must have stepped away from her chair.

"Just over to the clinic. We'll check you out, contact your party, make sure you're all right." He's very bouncy when he walks, like he's got springs in his shoes. He leads me to a golf cart that's bigger than the guest ones and motorized, I think. I get into the passenger seat, and he starts driving.

A few minutes later we arrive at a little cabin behind another cabin, and I feel like I need to lie down. Not because I feel sick. Just overwhelmed. *Nineteen eighty-two? That's thirty-two years ago.*

"My name is Ed, by the way."

"Hey, Ed, I'm Haley."

"Like the comet? That's a unique name. Nice to meet you, Haley." He opens the cabin door for me. Inside, it's nice and cold. There's an

AC unit rattling in the corner of the room. "Go ahead through that other door right there and lie down on the cot. Nurse Thomas will be with you in a moment."

"Thanks," I say, finding my way over to a cot covered in white butcher paper. I lie down on the crinkly bed. I shouldn't be here. They're going to ask me a bunch of questions I'm not going to be able to answer. I don't know where my parents are; I don't know where I'm staying, nor how I got here. They're just going to chalk it up to epilepsy disorientation and hold me until they can find my parents.

Which they won't.

So I never should've come here.

Nurse Thomas, I suppose, walks in, closes the door, and smiles. She's an older woman, and she's wearing a white dress with white shoes like in the old days. Well, that makes sense. "Hi, Haley. What brings you to us today?"

"I . . . uh . . . think I had a seizure. I mean, I've had one only once before, but I really feel fine now. I don't think I need to be here."

She reaches over and touches my forehead. "When was your last episode?"

"March. I'm just tired."

Then she pulls a thin glass tube out of a standing red container, wipes it clean, then shakes it several times. She turns to me. "Open."

I open my mouth, and she places it underneath my tongue. It smells of rubbing alcohol. "Close." I wait there with this glass thermometer, I guess, in my mouth for what I swear seems like five minutes. It never beeps, and I'm starting to think I have a fever of 125 degrees, it takes so long. Finally, she takes it out, examines it, and shrugs. "Ninety-eight. You're fine."

You mean I waited all that time for a normal reading?

"So tell me, dear, what were you doing before you passed out?" she asks, a polite smile across her face. I don't know why I'm intimidated by her. Maybe because she's wearing light blue eye shadow all over her lids.

"I was just swimming." Yes, it's a lie, but I can't quite tell her I was trespassing on abandoned, private territory.

"Did you feel light-headed or get the sense of déjà vu?"

All the standard seizure questions my doctors asked me. "Yes."

"Okay, well, go ahead and rest while we try to find your parents. Any idea where they might be? River Country, still, I would imagine?"

Time to lie, Haley. "Yes. Well, actually, my mom returned to the cabin to get my medication. She said she'll be right here."

"Cabin? You mean trailer."

"Yes, trailer."

"Oh." Nurse Thomas looks pleased that she won't have as much work to do as she thought. "Okay, well, that certainly makes things easier. What medication are you on?"

"I don't remember." It's Tegretol, but I want her to go away. I throw my arm over my forehead. "I'm just tired."

"Of course, dear. Just lie there and relax. I'll be right outside the room if you need me." She smiles, and I can tell she might have been pretty once. My leg is bouncing like crazy. I look around the room. There're two windows flanked with brown wilderness-print curtains; a few framed pictures of Mickey Mouse dressed as Davy Crockett, holding a rifle; a brown cabinet; and a watercooler with paper cups.

There's also a door to the outside with a dead bolt. *Note to self.*

I reach over, pull down a paper cup, and fill it with the best water I have ever drunk in my life. I didn't realize how thirsty I was, with all that's going on. I fill the cup three more times. I may need to employ the services of that door, even though it's probably locked. I can't stay here. My fake mother is never coming to bring me fake medicine. They're not going to find records of my family here.

I need to leave.

In the other room, I hear the medic and the nurse talking quietly. "They said she appeared out of nowhere. Nobody saw her slide down the slide. I know, it is strange."

"It's odd that her mother wouldn't bring her in, don't you think?"

Yes, I agree it's all very strange. I understand it even less than they do.

Nurse Thomas pokes her head into the room. "Haley, are you staying at Fort Wilderness, or were you just visiting River Country for the day?"

Hmm, I didn't know you could visit River Country for the day. I wonder if that would absolve me of having to explain what trailer I should be registered to. "We were just visiting family that's staying here." Wow, this lie is getting bigger and bigger, I'd say.

"I see. Would you happen to know whose name the registration might be under?"

"Petersen?" I mean, if my dad is here, he's probably with Anma and Ampa, but holy cow, I shouldn't have said that. What if they call my grandfather to come and identify me? He wouldn't know me from any other stowaway roaming around the campgrounds.

"Petersen," she repeats, and I think I hear the medic punching in numbers on a desk phone.

No, I can't stay here. "Where's the bathroom?" I ask. If I can't escape through a bathroom window, I'll just fake her into thinking I'm in the bathroom, then try that outside door and hope it's unlocked. Where would I even go? Ugh, I am the worst escape artist ever.

"It's right back there, dear, across from the closet."

"Okay, thank you," I call out. I head back there to check it out, but a few seconds later I hear a knock on the examining room door, even though it's open. I turn my head and see Jason looking into the room.

"Hi there," he says, all tanned and summery.

"Hey."

"Can I come in?"

"Yeah, yeah . . . come on in."

"How are you feeling?"

"I'm good, I'm good." I come back and sit down on the cot. "Listen," I whisper, "I really don't need to be here. I think I'm just going to leave. I really am feeling fine. Seriously, this happens all the time. Do you think you could tell her that you found my parents outside, and that I don't need to stay here?"

He seems to have forgotten his Disney responsibilities and is listening to me like any other friend of mine. Which is what I need. "I could, but are your parents really here?"

"No, but . . ." He's nineteen. I'm sure he understands what it's like getting in trouble. "Look, my dad would get really mad if he knew I was sliding down a slide when I'm not supposed to, so I don't want them to know about this."

His face reflects his confliction. "Okay, let me see what I can do." He gets up, but turns to me and whispers, "If we don't talk again now, look for me outside the pizza parlor at Pioneer Hall."

"Why wouldn't we talk again now?" I ask, but he is already out of the room, nearly closing the door behind him. "When do I meet you?"

He doesn't answer. Ugh, and he can't text me!

In the reception room, I hear him talking to Nurse Thomas, but I can't tell what they're talking about with the door almost completely closed. Then the door is cracked open, and Jason's hand appears. He throws me something that lands on the butcher paper and gleams gold.

A key.

To the door! Right!

I shoot off the bench over to the exterior door, sliding the key into the keyhole. As quietly as humanly possible, while Jason talks Nurse Thomas's ear off, I turn the key and unlock the door. I hear

Jason talking louder at that moment. He even pops his head in, as if checking on me, saying, "Oh, no, she's sleeping. Yeah, she's dead asleep. Best if we leave her alone."

I almost laugh out loud, but it gives me just the time I need to place the key on the cabinet and slip out the door. As soon as I'm out in the sunshine again, I breathe a huge sigh of relief, until I see—guess who?—my grandfather, Ampa, younger and really handsome, walking toward the cabin escorted by a Disney cast member. He's coming to see the girl claiming to be staying with the Petersen family.

Holy crap, I am out! I run in the direction of Pioneer Hall. There's a crowd of people hanging out on the veranda, kicking back in rocking chairs, and I throw myself into the middle of them, where I hope I can blend in better. That was close. Will they come looking for me? Hopefully, they'll just chalk it up to a girl who didn't want to be there. I sit here, people watching while I wait for Jason. It's hard to appreciate the thirty-year difference around me when Pioneer Hall looks pretty much the same now as it does in the future. It was designed to look like the eighteen hundreds, so it's all sort of timeless.

Classic, like the way I just escaped the clutches of Nurse Thomas. I must remember to thank Jason when I see him. I wait in a rocking chair, watching feathered hairstyle after feathered hairstyle pass me by. I see three rainbow-striped dresses, a dozen boys with socks up to their knees, and lots and lots of headbands on girls. *What* is that all about?

It's like old photo albums of my mom's come to life. I take it all in, and for the first time since awaking in River Country, I relax into an easy smile.

Two teen girls who come to sit in the rocking chairs next to me are giggling while looking at a hot pink, yellow, and black magazine—*Tiger Beat*. The guy posing on the front with his arms crossed looks like Superman's dad in *Smallville*, but younger and way more blond.

One of the girls looks up at me and freezes. "Sandra?" She reaches out to touch my arm.

I'm startled. "Me? No, Haley."

Her eyes, it's like they're staring right through me—hazel, almond shaped, cute, small nose, squarish jaw. There is no mistaking her. I have to do everything in my power to fight back the rising wave in my throat or throw my arms around her. It's those timeless, smooth photos of her come to life. Does she realize it's me?

Mommy?

seven

"I am so sure!" my super-young mom says, our eyes locked, her face frozen in permanent astonishment.

"Jenni, what is it?" Her friend volleys looks between me and her, but the more I check her out as well, the more I realize it's Lizzie, my mom's cousin.

"Doesn't she look exactly like my sister?" Mom asks. She's talking about my aunt, Sandra, who I guess must've been in college around this time. "I mean she totally looks like Sandy, big-time. Look at her!"

Lizzie stares at me. She looks nothing like her future self. She's always so mature hot, so MILFy. Here, she looks like such a geek. Poor thing! "Don't be an airhead, Jenni. She looks nothing like your sister. Your sister doesn't have those red streaks in her hair. Plus, she's, like, twenty-two."

"I didn't say they were the same age!" my mom bites back.

"Oh my God, don't have a cow. I'm just saying. Are those streaks natural? How did you get those?" Lizzie asks. They both stand there gaping at me.

I can't answer. On the inside, I'm bursting with joy that my mom is here too. Both of them! My parents! God, why am I so friggin' happy about this? I want to hug her, but I manage the best composure of my life instead. "Uh, no. They're highlights."

"Highlights?" my mom repeats, like it's a new concept. "Wow. They're so . . ." She waits for the right word to pop into her brain. "Punk! I love them."

Punk? I look punk to my mom? *Ha-ha*, that's so cute. "Thanks. My name is Haley, by the way. Not Sandy." I laugh nervously. But not too much. Just in case she recognizes me. Which is impossible. "I'll see you around later?"

"Fer sure," fifteen-year-old Mom says.

"Totally," Lizzie agrees, thrilled, it seems, that an older girl wants to hang out with them. They decide to move to another spot, taking looks back at me, and I wait until they disappear before letting go of a huge breath, wondering what the hell just hit me.

I almost text Jason to let him know what happened and ask where he is, then I remember yet AGAIN that I can't text. Damn! How did people meet in public places in the old days? Stop and yell out to each other?

I'm about to get up and go look for him when I hear, "Hello." Jason startles the crap out of me. I notice my mom and Lizzie still looking at me from the other end of the veranda. Now they're probably wondering how did I get so lucky to have cute towel guy talk to me.

"Hey there, you," I say, looking up at him. "Thanks for bailing me out back there."

"Oh, it's cool. I get it. I wouldn't want my old man coming down on me either. Wanna get something to eat?"

"Yeah, sure, but, uh, I didn't bring any money."

He points to his Disney name tag. "I know people. Come on." I get out of the chair, and we walk into the pizza place past a cute, smiling brown-haired hostess.

"Howdy, Jason," she coos.

"Hey, Mabel." He smiles back.

"Anywhere you like, sugar." She's easily in her early twenties and probably doubles as Snow White in Fantasyland when she's not here, she's that perfect. Did she just call him *sugar*?

"Thanks."

Hmm, I think Marsha was right about the swooning girls at every turn.

We stride along the dark wood floors to a table next to a window, where we sit down. In the back, there're a bunch of arcade games, with several kids waiting at each one, not being ignored like they would in the future. Pac-Man, Space Invaders, something called Centipede, others called Donkey Kong, Frogger, and Galaga. How would I know to dream about these games if I've never seen some of them before?

I look at Jason.

He looks at me.

This could get very awkward. Or he could be my liaison to navigating this world if I play my cards right. "So . . . ," I begin.

"So, I guess you met Marsha."

"Marsha? Oh, the girl in the red bikini? Yeah. She's nice."

"She's my brother's girlfriend. At least he sees her that way."

Whoa. "Wait, you mean she's not with that other guy back there?" My dad. I know it's not true, but I throw it out there just to see what he says.

"Oscar?" He smiles, shaking his head. "Nah. The dude's cool, but he doesn't have a clue. She's not into him at all. She has the hots for my brother. We all hang out during summers here, though."

The hots. I guess he means she thinks his brother is hot. *Aww, poor Dad!* Wait . . . we? So Jason and my dad used to hang? An older waitress saunters over. Jason orders a large pepperoni pizza and a pitcher of Coke. He folds his hands in front of him. He smiles his cute, crooked smile. "So, Haley, Haley, Haley."

"Jason, Jason, Jason." I fold my hands like him. I know that whatever is coming is going to focus largely on me.

"I'm a bit baffled. Was hoping maybe you could help me out," he says, his blue eyes darker now by the window shade.

I knew it. He wants to conduct an interrogation, not get to know me better. Well, I did appear out of nowhere. I guess I'm just as strange to him as his world is to me. "You're wondering where I came from," I say.

"That . . . is the understatement of the year." He nods, smirking.

"Try looking at it my way. A teenage girl is dragged out of the water semiconscious. She's in regular clothes instead of a bathing suit, which, I must admit, was . . . quite disappointing." He turns up a mischievous grin.

I smile and glance down at the table.

"She wakes up, confused about where she is. I can accept that. But then she can't find anyone she knows, has this little machine she calls an 'eye-phone,' and she says weird things that make no sense." He laughs and sits back. "So far, I'm thinking you fell out of an episode of *Star Trek*."

I sigh. "It's a phone. The little machine is called a cell phone. Here, look." I pull it out of my pocket and place it in front of him. I press the button to wake it up, but nothing happens. "Wait, sometimes it does this. Maybe it's wet."

Damn it, don't tell me. . . . I press the button harder. Nothing. Ack! My phone's battery sucks!

"So you mean to tell me that you have a telephone you carry around with you everywhere. How does it work without a cord? Where would you even get something like that? Your old man's Double-O-Seven?"

"No," I say. *My dad is that clueless kid trying to pick up your brother's girlfriend out there.* I smack my phone a few times. "It's dead. I can't show you. The battery must have run out." I can't believe this. Now I'm without my charger in a time where chargers don't exist. Fabulous. Tell me, exactly *how* am I supposed to survive?

"That's not thick enough for batteries." I look up, and he's staring at me pretty hard. He's really trying to work this all out in his head but could never, ever imagine the whole truth.

I have to just go with it.

Maybe I will wake up. Or maybe my dream will shift to another year. But for now, I have to accept that it's not, that it *is* 1982, and *I* am the fish out of water here. But I can't tell him when I'm from either. He would inform his lifeguard brother, and the word would get out that there's a raving lunatic roaming Fort Wilderness. So I *need* to lie as low as possible until I figure out how to get back.

"Okay, look," I say, letting go of a huge sigh. "My dad is . . . an inventor." Not true, of course, but perfect. "He builds all kinds of things, and I, you know, test them out for him."

"Oh." He sits back in his chair and folds his hands again in front of him. "Now you're starting to make sense. So he made that thing? Well, that's pretty good for a home-cooked invention. How did he get that silver apple so smooth on the back like that? Does he work for Apple Computer or something?"

"No, he doesn't work for—wait, you know about Apple?" I'm not a computer-history buff or anything, but I thought Apple started around the time I was born. Or maybe I'm clueless.

"Well, they're not like Commodore's computers or the TRS-80, but I've heard of them. Hey, ask your dad if he knows anything about the Commodore 64 that's coming out next month. That's supposed to be really killer. I can't wait for it."

"Yeah. Killer. I . . ." I have no clue what he's talking about. "I will. I'll ask him." I smile.

His face lights up suddenly. "So rad if he had photos of one. I love getting sneak peeks at stuff before they come out. Every year when the *TV Guide Fall Preview* comes out with descriptions of the new shows starting, I rush out to get one. That's one of the reasons why I applied to work here this summer."

"Because you love *TV Guide?*" *What even is* TV Guide?

He laughs. "You're real funny. You don't come to Disney often, do you?"

"Actually, I've come a bunch of times. Why?"

"Then you should know what we're all waiting for around here. The Experimental Prototype Community of Tomorrow?" His eyebrows raise, full of hope that I'm as excited as he is. "Opening October first?" A crooked smile and sideways glance test my knowledge of insider Disney information. Which is completely blank at the moment.

"Maybe I'm still a little disoriented?"

"EPCOT Center!" he cries, his smile as goofy as a little kid getting a new game system. "The new Disney park! They just finished the new monorail that extends that way. It's a two-and-a-half-mile trip. The new trains are so sleek. We got to preview them before the public does. They took cast members on a tour of Future World. You would not believe some of the inventions they have there— these computers that you can touch the screen and choose different options, and it responds to your fingertip! It is the coolest technology you have ever seen! It's incredible!"

"No way!" I sit back and pretend it's really amazing to hear about stuff that's been around forever. "That is really awesome!"

"Yeah," he says, genuinely happy. "Awesome."

Good thing my phone battery is dead, or else he'd be more fascinated by it than by me.

The waitress brings over the pitcher of soda and pours us two cups full of ice. "Jason?" She nods at his tag, still pinned to his shirt.

He looks down. "Oh." And removes it. "I'm not a cast member right now," he whispers. "In fact, cast members aren't supposed to eat here, but they know I'm staying through the summer, so it's not like I can eat anywhere else."

I take a big gulp of my Coke. It's sweet, icy cold, and perfect. "What do you mean? You live in Fort Wilderness too?" Who knew so many people spent the summer here?

"Not all year, no. But they always need extra help during peak season, so my brother and I applied to River Country, and we got the jobs. Which brings me to another question. Why haven't you told your family yet about what happened to you? I still haven't seen you with anyone. It's really strange to see guests on their own, especially kids."

Kids? I know he's older than me, but it's not like he's not a kid himself.

"I was afraid you'd notice that." Maybe this was a bad idea to come and meet him.

His eyes soften. He gets that look again, where's he's not an employee at the moment, just a friend. He leans closer to me across the table. "Do they know you're here, Haley?"

If I say no, his sense of cast member responsibility might kick back in, and he'll try to get me reunited with my nonexistent family. If I say yes, he'll want to see them.

At that exact moment a steaming pepperoni pizza is set on the table between us, along with two metal plates. Thank God the American pioneers of the Ol' West knew how to make pizza, because I am starving! "Let's eat!" I reach for a slice.

But Jason's expression looks like he thinks he's figured it out. "You could eat this whole pizza pie, couldn't you?" He checks under the table, then back at me. "You swiped those sandals, and you could use new shorts. Haley, I promise I won't tell anybody. I'm not a cast member right now, okay? Who let you in?"

Who let me in? I chuckle and put down the slice. "It's not what you think. I'm not a runaway. My parents know I'm here."

"Yeah? Then where are they?"

"Okay." I watch the swirling lines of steam rising from the melted mozzarella. "Promise me you won't freak out."

"You mean flip out."

"Whatever." I play around with the Parmesan cheese shaker. "Consider this one of my dad's experiments. Kind of like a dare. What happened was, we got into an argument. He said I didn't appreciate him, my little brother and sister, so they left. Without me. Like, teaching me a lesson."

"That sounds unusually cruel."

"It's not. My dad is always doing stuff like that. He wants to show me what it's like to get along in the world without him. He's just trying to get me to understand. Now I have to figure out where I'm going to sleep, how I'm going to eat without any money. See? Teaching me a lesson."

"But you suffer from seizures. No father would do that."

Crap. He's right. This lie totally sucks! *Modify.*

"You wouldn't think so, but they didn't leave Disney World. They just moved to the Contemporary for the rest of the week. He's waiting to see how long before I give up, go back to him, beg for forgiveness, you know? But I know he's keeping an eye on me. Fact, I saw him a little while ago. He doesn't know I saw him though."

Please, Jason. Please buy this whole story. It's gotten way better! And part of it is true.

He winces, points to the pizza, and says, "You're not eating. Sounds fishy, Haley. But I guess some parents are modern like that. What are you going to do? Seems like he's right. You can survive in the campground without a roof over your head, but you can't survive without cash." He serves himself, then digs in. "I mean, let's face it. This *is* Disney."

He's right. And I feel like Pinocchio for stretching this lie as far as it will go. But Dina did say I could get anything I wanted by using my looks. Maybe I need to use that advantage now.

I pick up the slice again and try not to shove the entire thing down my throat, as hungry as I am. "Right, so I was thinking . . . maybe you could help me with that?" I tilt my face ever so cutely to one side, as cutely as one can appear while swallowing huge mouthfuls of pizza.

I know this is terrible. Jason really is, quite possibly, the nicest guy I have met in a long time, and I feel horrible for fooling him. But I need a place to sleep, clothes to wear, and food to eat. This dream-hallucination has not exempted me from needing the basics. I need his help until I figure out how to get back to the twenty-first century. If I have to stress myself out to trigger another seizure, that's what I'll do. Problem is, what if I don't go back to the present after doing so? What if I fall into a different year altogether?

Man, how does the Doctor deal with this?

"Haley, I want to help you, but I can't just show up with this homeless girl and ask my dad if you can stay in our motor home. First off, there's no room, and second, how would that look?"

"I understand." I'm suddenly not very hungry anymore. What did I expect? "I'll just take the next boat to the Contemporary and find my father. I appreciate everything you've done for me."

I wish it were that simple. When, really, my only choice is to hand myself over to authorities as soon as I'm done with this pizza. I can loiter around the campground for only so long before someone catches me foraging for food inside the trash bins. I'll have to come clean with my lunatic time-travel story, explain my medical history, and let them figure me out. At least I'll be safe and fed.

Jason says nothing, polishes off two more slices, and downs his soda while I sit there pecking at my slice. He watches me intently, shakes his head, and says, "I don't know what it is about you. But okay. You got me."

You got me—the sexiest words he's said so far. He's in! He's in my world, as much as I'm in his. At Jason's mercy isn't such a bad place to be. I look up, holding down my happiness. "So you'll help me?"

A smile materializes across his face. He signals for the waitress to come over, then asks for a check. A girl older than me strolls right through the restaurant, flipping her long headbanded hair in Jason's direction. She's hot, and the way he looks at her for a split second makes my stomach flip. Because everyone seems to notice Jason. But he's chosen to spend his time with me. "Yes. But if I get in trouble for this, you owe me."

I bounce in my seat, smiling at him. "I owe you, no matter what."

eight

As great as it's been meeting Jason, there's a huge downside to all this.

My future dad is wondering where I am by now.

He's probably already notified Disney security. They're scouring the campground right at this very moment. It might even be morning, since it's turning to dusk around here. Then again, do I exist in the future if I'm here now? The thought makes my stomach hurt.

Jason weaves his cart through the streets with the same expertise Dina did yesterday, if you can call it "yesterday." And he's right. There are no log cabins now. Just loop after loop of trailers all in a row. On the seat between us is a folded-up newspaper—the *Orlando Sentinel*. The date—July first, 1982. There's a review for the movie *Blade Runner* on it: "Futuristic Thriller Fails to Make the Cut."

Wow. The cult classic my dad's always talking about? Got a bad review? *For shame, Father.* I want to take a picture but remember the dead battery. *Ergh.* Mental picture instead.

"So you came to enjoy the Fourth of July weekend and ended up getting in a fight with your old man instead. That stinks. Where you all from, anyway?" he asks.

"Jupiter." Ugh, that was supposed to be Atlanta!

"Jupiter, neat. I've driven through there a few times," he says, making no joke about my town's name being the same as a planet in our solar system like every other person always seems to. "And you're a what? Junior? Senior?"

"I'll be starting my senior year."

He nods, pressing his lips together. I'm not sure what that means, whether he's disappointed that I'm still in high school, or whether he's happy we're close in age.

"What about you?" I play with the frayed hem of my shorts.

"I don't know yet what I'm going to do," he says pensively.

"You're not in college?"

"I don't know if college is right for me. I was thinking the army might be better."

"Wait, what? Why don't you think college is right for you?"

"'Cause. I don't know. I thought maybe I'd keep working for Disney, maybe climb the ranks, since my foot's already in the door. That's sort of always been my dream. But we'll see."

What he's saying makes me sad. I mean, he seems pretty smart. He would make a good computer programmer, engineer, or something. I'm pretty sure you can't do that without a degree. Part of me feels relieved, though. At the thought that if I stay here, he won't be leaving for college right away. Though what business I have thinking we might have an attraction or that I might be staying here is just bizarre. No, my goal is definitely to wake up or find my way home.

"Is that a bad thing?" he asks, turning down a street named Terry Trail. "Not having any aspirations? I guess that must sound lame to you."

"No. I think for some people it's normal not to know what you're going to do after high school. But had you gone to my school, they would've pounded you into a career path before graduation. My school is all about focus, focus, focus." Maybe that's a generational thing. Maybe they didn't have career fairs, FCAT, and IB programs in 1982.

"Well, that's sort of why I was hoping to join the army. I could learn a thing or two while figuring out what I want to study."

"I guess that might work." It occurs to me suddenly that Jason must be alive somewhere in the future, working for the army. He's three years older than my dad. Common sense is screaming the word *illegal* at my brain, so I should therefore abandon any thoughts of romance. But when I look at the kid sitting next to me at the wheel, that's all I really see—a kid. Older than me, yes, but only by two years.

Because here's another thought . . . what if I'm not dreaming? In the future I might be a missing person right now, while my parents kill each other over whose fault it is. But here, now, life continues. With Mom, Dad, Erica, Willy, and Alice there. And me here.

I may be stuck here.

Jason makes a turn by a trailer with a big American flag in the front window and stops in front of a beige trailer with a red racing stripe across the middle. "Well, this is it. You can stay here for now, two days tops, or until you think your dad has learned his lesson." He smiles, then looks down at his feet. "But, uh, Haley, you're going to have to go back eventually. You know that, right?"

He has no idea. "Yes, I know. Whose trailer is this? I don't feel right intruding on—"

"No one," he interrupts. "It's empty. I mean, you might find my brother trying to get in without the key, but I'm going to do everything I can to prevent that." He sees my momentary confusion, as I try to figure out why he would have a key to an empty trailer, then leans against the siding. "Geez, this is embarrassing."

"Oh," I say, clucking my tongue. "I got it."

This makes him look even more perplexed, as if a girl shouldn't understand anything about guys sharing a private place, a booty place, to be more specific. "Nah, I don't think you do. It's guy stuff. You wouldn't—"

"First of all, I might be a girl, but I get it. Second, you don't have to explain anything to me. It's none of my business."

He shakes his head. "Now, don't go thinking it's mine, because it's not."

"Of course not. You just hold the keys for your brother, right?"

I chide, but somewhere inside I do feel a little jealous of all the girls he's probably brought here, even though he denies it. Why that should bother me, I don't know. Maybe I wanted to believe that Jason was different. Call me crazy.

He looks genuinely offended. "As a matter of fact, I do. The raccoons that live out here are more responsible than he is. One day they'll drain River Country and find all of Jake's dropped keys and lifeguard whistles sitting there at the bottom of the lagoon." He laughs, then runs up the steps to unlock the trailer.

His words sting. Not because I care about his brother, but because it'll happen. River Country will cease to be. He can't even imagine what I saw. It's frustrating knowing a world of information I can't share with him. Not only would I ruin his vision of the future if I did, but it'd ruin our relationship, too. And even though I know I shouldn't start one, I don't want any ruination of one just yet.

The trailer is laid out pretty much the same as the cabins that replace them, with kitchen, bunk beds, bathroom, and everything else. "I'll get you some clothes from the trading post, enough to last a couple of days. What, uh, size are you?" he asks.

"A four if it's shorts, a small or medium if it's shirts."

"You know what?" He pulls out his wallet and hands me a fifty-dollar bill. "This should get you a few things. They might have Fort Wilderness logos on them, but at least you won't look like a castaway anymore." He smiles so sweetly, I want to run my hand along his face.

I stare down at the money. This is nice of him. "Jason, I don't feel right."

"Just take it, Haley. Your dad can pay me back. Or better yet, get me the insider scoop on that new Commodore 64. Listen, I have to go check in with my folks. But I'll be back soon. Don't go sliding off slides by yourself, okay?" Blue eyes and dimples send me swooning.

"I'll be fine. I'll take the bus to Pioneer Hall, the campfire, or something. I won't be alone. Don't worry. Go do whatever you gotta do." I'm shooing him away, but I really want him to come back. He's kind of grown on me. I would definitely spend more time with him if I were in the future. But I'm not. So this needs to stay friendly.

"There's no bus. You gotta take the tram. Okay, but if I don't see you again later, look for me tomorrow by River Country. I'm always there," he says, and my heart falls a little. I was kind of hoping he'd come back later and, I don't know . . . hang out with me . . . or something.

Because now that I think about it, I may not be here tomorrow. I may not be here tonight. But I can't hang out with him. I really have to figure out how to get home. "Of course. Go. I'll see you tomorrow."

I can feel him thinking the same by the way he's blinking slowly. Maybe he's wondering if he'll see me again. "Hey, you said your birthday was coming up," he says, leaning back against the door. "I remember because you wanted your dad to buy you something. . . ."

An iPad. I nod. "Yeah, good memory."

"So you'll be how old?" Ah. A guy doesn't ask how old you are unless he's having thoughts of hooking up with you. At least I hope that's what he's thinking.

"Eighteen."

He closes his eyes for a second, and maybe it's just me, but he seems really relieved. "Eighteen. Okay. Rad."

"Rad. Okay, Jason-Jason."

He smiles that wide, gorgeous smile of his. "All right, Haley-Haley." His gaze lingers on me a moment. Then he taps the door frame, scuttles down the steps, and drives off in his cart.

I lean against the railing with butterflies in my stomach and watch him go. He's really cute. Like, really cute. But NO . . . I can't.

I close the door and scan the trailer. How plain can you get? Hey, at least the AC is running. I need a nap. I feel like I've been awake for days. Yet I'm terrified to drift off. Do I really want to sleep in a bed that Jake brings girls to? But more important, what if I wake up back in the present?

And then I'll never know.

How this dream—this crazy time-travel hallucination where I met a really sweet guy one summer in 1982—was ever supposed to end.

nine

Exhaustion catches up with me, and I sleep on the couch until it's dark out. I have no idea what time it is when I wake up. The day's events come back to haunt me. Waking up on the beach, my tongue hurting, realizing where I am . . . *when* I am. I'm stuck in the past, with nothing but a dead cell phone and fifty borrowed bucks.

Part of me wants to get up and join the world. Another part of me, the part that's winning, wants to keep sleeping. I'm vaguely aware of my muscles. I'm sore and probably bruised. Did I really slide down a waterslide when I passed out? Was it the action of sliding that got me here, or the seizure itself, regardless of where it happened?

Thinking about it makes me doze off again. I'm not hungry nor do I have any desire to get up. I just sleep. And dream about an empty baseball diamond as the sun descends into an orange field. A dream within a dream. And of my dad sitting up late into the night, regretting letting me drive off alone, hoping to see his baby girl one more time.

There's a knock on a metal door. Again, and again. I hear it for a while before I realize it's not a dream. My eyes pop open. "Haley?" Someone's calling me from outside. Then, a sharper tap on the window. "Haley, you in there?"

I stumble to my feet. Feels like someone hit me over the head with a two-by-four. "Coming," I mumble. Where am I again?

"Haley?" He doesn't hear me.

"I'm coming, I'm coming." I shuffle over to the door in the darkness and peer out the window. Jason—now I remember. He's in his River Country uniform, holding a drink cup and some clothes. From the lavender-and-golden sky outside, it looks to be about dusk, the same time he dropped me off. So I must've slept only a few minutes. I open the door.

"Well, good morning, sunshine." He's looking fresh and gorgeous as ever. He hands me the cup and what appears to be a folded shirt and shorts. "You want some Coke? Those are my mom's, by the way. I need them back." He switches on a lamp, and I'm almost blinded.

"Thanks." I take the cup and let him in. I sip the Coke, plopping back down on the couch. "How long was I asleep?"

He sits on the edge of the couch cautiously, as though gauging whether the proximity would bother me. "I don't know. What time did you go to sleep?" he asks.

"Right after you dropped me off."

His eyes and mouth fly open. "You've been asleep since yesterday? Holy crap, woman!"

"I have? I guess my body needed to recover," I mumble. My stomach feels tight and rumbly. "Yesterday? Really?" I wince at him.

He nods. "You must be starving. I'll go get you something to eat. Unless you want to keep me company."

As much as I want to go with Jason and have another bite to eat, the thought of my dad, and maybe even my mom by now, worrying about where I am slaps me back to reality. *I can't, Jason. I have to go home now*, I want to say. Somehow I have to make it happen. "How about I meet you near Pioneer Hall later. Or wherever you'll be," I tell him.

"Sounds good. The shower works, by the way, and there's toothpaste and an extra toothbrush in the bathroom." He points down the hall of the trailer.

I smile at him softly. "Thanks. You've been really nice."

"Hey . . ." He peers into my face. "You okay?"

"Yeah, I'm just . . . I don't know how much longer I can be here. I think my dad might be worried." I press my palms against my forehead and rub the sleep out of my eyes.

"I can imagine." He's quiet for a minute. "A daughter that looks like you. I'd be terrified."

I look at him. "What do you mean?"

"Well, I'd flip if you were my daughter. I mean, look at you. It's not like you're hard on the eyes. Any number of sickos would love to get their hands on you. It's scary."

His words pierce my heart. They really hurt. One, because my dad would never have left me on my own, but it was the only story I could think of. Two, because he thinks that of my dad, and three, because my father is probably fearing the worst right now. It's not fair to keep him waiting like this.

I can tell this isn't easy for Jason, either. On one hand, he probably wants to do the right thing by getting me back to my family, and on the other, he seems to like me, as much as I like him, and probably wants me to stay. "I'll find you later, after I've had a chance to freshen up. Is that cool?"

He smiles and stands up. "Cool. See you later, Haley-Haley."

"Jason-Jason."

I think he's lingering, maybe to see what my next move will be. It really kills me, because in a different time, I would've made the next move and maybe even kissed him. But it's not the right time, nor place. "Thanks for the drink. And the clothes," I say, holding them up in my hand.

"I hope they fit."

We stand there a moment more looking at each other, and it occurs to me that I may not see him again. If I find my way home tonight, that is. I record his face in my mind so I can always remember the boy who went out of his way to help me. Then, I lace an arm around his neck and hug him hard, feeling his arms squeezing me back.

After a moment he slips away down the steps to his cart. "Later, Haley."

"Bye," I whisper.

I close the door behind him.

Don't cry. Do not.

I unfold the clothes. There're a pair of pink elastic-waist shorts, a Mickey Mouse T-shirt, and something else that falls to the floor. I pick it up. A pair of white panties. Ha-ha. I can imagine Jason's mortification at rifling through his mom's stuff just so I would have something clean to wear. They smell like someone else's drawer. Clean, but not mine. Better than me right now, that's for sure.

I take a long shower, letting the hot water rinse the soreness away, and towel off in the dark brown-and-beige bathroom. It looks so old, but it serves its purpose. His mother's clothes fit me okay. The shirt fits fine, but the shorts are a little tight. I decide to keep the underwear on but to wear my shorts instead.

I pocket my dead cell phone and venture outside, leaving the key to the trailer underneath the mat. Logical enough place for Jason or Jake to find it again. I have the fifty-dollar bill in my pocket in case I need it. My stomach is really rumbling now. Maybe I should've gone to eat.

Too late.

In the hot evening, I walk to the nearest station and wait for the silent tram to arrive. It's full of people returning to the Magic Kingdom for the nighttime parade and fireworks, I'm guessing, since we've done the same so many times. I hop in and enjoy the whoosh of the silent takeoff. We snake through the streets until we reach the Pioneer Hall station.

I jump off the tram and stand there, as everyone else around me walks ahead. Where exactly was I when I fell through time? Standing at the top of the Whoop 'n' Holler slide in River Country. I have to make it back there.

I have to try to make a seizure happen in the same place again. Maybe there was a—what do you call it?—like, a vortex of energy there. I've heard of places like that, where there're extraordinary amounts of energy, and strange things happen in these spots. Maybe if I re-create the same conditions, it'll happen. I know it sounds crazy, but it's the most logical solution I can think of right now.

Except I can't just walk into River Country. It's closed now. I could go in the same way I did the first time, swimming through the lake. But it seems to me there're easily five times as many people here today than there are in the future. I guess River Country kept the campground busier in general.

To my left there's a petting zoo, and behind that a service road. A truck is turning into the road. It seems to lead behind Pioneer Hall, which means behind River Country. I check around to make sure no one is looking, then run through the petting zoo under the curious stares of chicken and sheep.

A little goat saunters up to me. I pat him on the head but keep moving. There's a noise behind a shed. I run to the edge of a barn to hide. Someone is walking out with someone else, a man and a woman, in blue plaid shirts, talking about what they overheard some guest say earlier. They don't see me.

I bust through to the back edge of the petting zoo, straddle the wooden fence, and climb out onto the service road. The truck I saw before is up ahead, stopped, with lights on. The driver is hanging out the window talking loudly and laughing with someone throwing away garbage behind Pioneer Hall.

"Later."

"Later, buddy!"

I need an excuse in place in case someone finds me snooping. My only defense is to say I got lost and ended up here quite by accident. Scooting along the road, I pray I don't run into anybody, and eventually I reach a fenced-in area that says KEEP OUT. I've become quite the professional trespasser!

Behind it are the sounds of motors and machines, and I see the back-side, concave openings of the rock boulders from River Country. They hide water pipes and pumps. Leave it to Disney to make the world a stage. Great, so I got this far. But now I have to venture inside without anyone seeing me.

I hear employees inside, moving around, banging garbage containers, the swish-swishing of water being moved around by pipes, brooms, and who knows what. I'm behind the chlorinated pool with the two steep slides, but I can't get in through here. I have to keep moving down this street. It's hard to know exactly where you are when you've seen a place only once, but *if* I remember correctly, the Whoop 'n' Holler slides are farther down that way.

My nerves are on high alert. I make it all the way to the end of the road without being noticed and slide through an open gate in the chain-link fence. Peering from behind a large reddish rock, I see someone coming carrying garbage bags. I scoot back behind a recess. *Please, please don't see me. Keep moving. . . .*

I hear the fence gate close, then the sound of a Dumpster opening and closing. *Phew.*

To my right is the edge of Bay Lake. I'm close to the waterslide I need to find. But how do I get up there from here? I hope there's a way to access it that's not from the general-public side. Inching along the rock, I come around the curve and find a set of stairs roped off with a chain. CAST MEMBERS ONLY.

Why, that would be me. . . .

This is it. This leads to the top of the rock formation where I fell. Carefully, I step over the chain and head up the stairs. What if there's someone up there, cleaning? My heart beats in my throat, and I feel the saliva in my mouth turning hot, as if I'm going to throw up, but I don't feel a seizure coming on.

And, for once, I'm disappointed.

When I get to the top, I catch my breath and take in the view. It's easier to understand the layout of the park now that there's some light still left out. The winding slides are fresh and clean, not consumed by trees and dead leaves like when I last stood here. There's actually a sandy beach where there was nothing but shrubs and clumps of trees before. River Country employees are lining up the chairs nice and straight and getting the whole place ready for another day of fun tomorrow.

It's not a big water park like Blizzard Beach or Typhoon Lagoon, but it's quaint and private, and I can see how a kid—how anyone—could spend a whole day here *having a blast.*

I move over to the top of the slide, which now has a chain across it, too, closed for the evening. *Okay, universe, God, or whoever is in charge . . .* I hold on to the rock wall next to me and close my eyes, trying to feel the vibrations of this place. *I really like 1982, seems like a great time. But I've learned my lesson. So . . . can I go home now?*

Nothing happens. A warm breeze comes in from the lake, wrapping me in a summery glow, but that's it. *Please, this is killing my parents, I know it. I really like Jason and could definitely get to know him better, but . . . I need to go home.*

Nothing.

Maybe it needs to be nighttime. Maybe my cell phone, interference, or electrical stuff had something to do with it. My phone was on at the time. I slide it out of my pocket and try turning it on again.

Dead. Deader than an abandoned water park.

I sit down cross-legged in the spot I last remember before I fell. There was someone—a security guard, most likely—chasing me; I won't forget that.

I'm in the same spot I was two days ago but light-years away from home. Suddenly the stress of it all hits me. A wave of sadness rises into my throat. The anguish stings my eyes. Why is this happening to me? What do I have to do to get home? If my parents eventually accept that I'm missing or dead, how do I continue to live in this place and time?

Come on, seizures, when I finally need you for something, you're nowhere to be found!

Inadvertently, I kick on the fiberglass slide, and the sound carries a short way, like a muffled gong. A moment later it's like a genie appears behind me.

Except totally not a genie.

Jake's arms are crossed, his legs apart, like a genie, but that's it. "Well, look who we have here."

ten

I was just going," I say, getting up to leave, but Jake blocks my path.

"I don't think so. First you appear out of nowhere, then you escape the clinic and my boss made us all look for you, and now you show up here after the park is closed. I'd say it's time I made a call." He lifts his walkie-talkie to his mouth, but I grab his arm and pull him down.

"No, please. Listen, it's not what you think. Jake, right?" My eyes beg him to listen.

He glances at me sideways, unsure. "You've been hanging around my brother, haven't you? No wonder I couldn't find him anywhere after work yesterday." He scoffs and shakes his head.

"I know it looks like I'm trespassing, but there's a perfectly good explanation for it."

"Which is?"

"Which . . . I can't explain to you right now."

He lifts his walkie-talkie again, but I block him.

"I will. I'll explain soon, just please let me go. Don't call your manager." I look at him, and it's amazing how much he looks like Jason, but with darker hair, a mustache, and brown eyes. And an attitude a little more . . .

He presses the button on his walkie-talkie anyway. "This is Jake at RC. I have an unregistered guest wandering the facility." *Evil.*

"No!" I grab the walkie-talkie from his hand and hold it over the slide. He lunges forward to get it. "I'll drop it! I swear, I will."

"I could get in trouble if I lose that."

A voice crackles through the speaker. "Copy, Jake. Security will be right there. Name your location."

I pretend to fling the radio down the waterslide. "Don't tell them. I told you I had a good reason."

"I don't care what that reason is."

Great, now what? "Well, do you care that your girlfriend was hanging out with another guy yesterday while you were working?"

At this, he stops. His whole expression changes. "What do you mean? Oscar? He's just a friend."

"Are you sure?" I'm so using him. Of course he knows he's just a friend, but I hope I've given him enough to think about so he'll leave me alone. "I don't know, she really seemed to like him. I'm just sayin'."

"Give me the radio."

"Don't report me."

"I already did. They're on their way." Our eyes lock. I want to punch him for being such a jerk. "I had to, I'm sorry. I can't lose this job."

My eyes shoot mental fireballs at him. "Thanks a lot." I crouch down and hurl the walkie-talkie down the slide, hearing it make its way around the first bend. The water is turned off, but the slides are still wet enough for it to go winding its way around.

"No!" He jumps in after it, and I take advantage of the time it'll take him to catch it before it hits the lagoon and climb back up to run off.

Quickly, I hustle down the stairs and over to the gate I came through, but it's been locked tight with a chain. Ack! I climb the fence, curling my legs over the top edge, and jump down, losing a flip-flop on the other side. I reach under the fence to grab it, even though it's slowing me down. But I won't get far without shoes on boiling hot pavement.

Reach . . . and . . . got it!

Run. Run, Haley. . . .

I race down the service road, but halfway down I see a truck coming up the road. I duck behind some bushes next to a building behind the pool rock formation I saw when I first got here. There's another gate open, and a lady standing right there, cleaning the side-walk with a powerful spray hose. I stop to catch my breath for a second.

Her back faces me, and the hose is really loud, so I whisk right past her without her even noticing me. I'm in the bathroom and locker area. It's still inside the water park, where there's a network of sidewalks leading back to Pioneer Hall, but almost to the outside. No one notices me. Not one person.

Except my mom. Of course.

"Oh my gosh, you scared me." She turns around and holds her chest while leaning over. "Haley, right?"

What is she doing here? I'm pretty sure the front gate must be closed at this time. How did she get in? And how do I tell my past-mom I don't have time to talk to her?

I scan around, making sure Jake is not after me. "Yeah, Haley."

"I guess I wandered in here by accident. Oops! Where is the exit again?" She laughs nervously. My mom, trespassing too? I see how my straight-laced dad thought she was a little too adventurous. She could get in trouble! Where's my grandma if not watching her? "Hey, can I ask you something?" she says, leaning into me.

"Yeah, sure."

"I saw that you were having lunch with that guy from the towel shack. What's his name?"

Uh-oh. Don't tell me she likes him too. That would be too much. "Jason?"

"Right, Jason." She looks around, gathering her courage, then back at me. We walk to the front gate, which I see now was left ajar with a garbage can on wheels propping it open. "I guess that's why you were in here too, waiting for him to get off work, huh?"

Yes, let her think that. "Oh, sure, right."

"Well, do you know the guy that he and his brother sometimes spend time with? Medium height, brown hair, not his brother, but the other one?"

Aha. And so it begins.

I look at her fresh face, her beautiful mouth, her hair half picked up on the sides and held with two barrettes. I'm looking at the beginnings of me. Of Haley Petersen. I smile at her. "Yeah, Oscar. Oscar Petersen."

"Oscar Petersen," she says, trying the name out in her vocal repertoire. She pokes her head out the gate and opens it for us. "Come on, nobody's looking. Yeah, that one. He stays in my loop every year. He's so cute." It's almost as if she's forgotten that I'm standing right here with her.

"He is. He's perfect for you," I say, and she looks back at me and smiles giddily.

"You think? But he never even notices me. He's always with *that girl.*" She says *that girl* like Marsha is a bug that should be crushed.

"Oh, he will," I say, looking at the way those words seem to make her whole being come alive. A moment ago she wasn't sure of herself, and now I've made a goddess out of a geek. "He'll get over her, don't worry."

She stares at me in disbelief. "Wow. Thanks, Haley. You're a good friend. I know I've only known you a couple of days, but I don't know what it is. . . . It's like I've known you forever."

I guess, in some way, we have known each other forever. And always will. *I love you, Mommy.* "Me too. Some people just click like that, huh?" I smile.

"*Click*, yeah." She likes that word.

As much as I want to stand here talking to my mom, I have to move along. Jake could come running with security guards any moment now. A couple of cast members walk by the front entrance and glance our way, though they're gabbing too much to realize we shouldn't be here.

"We have to get out of here," I mumble, hurrying toward the exit. "Catch you around later?"

"Sure. Where will you be?"

"I don't know. Pioneer Hall maybe?"

"Well, I'm going back to Magic Kingdom with my family in a bit to see the fireworks. They're over at the marina about to get the launch. I was here hoping . . ." She smiles sheepishly. "To find Oscar. I know I shouldn't be." She laughs to herself. "But he's really cute. I just wanted to find him, thought he'd be with those guys who work here. You know what I mean?"

I nod. I totally know what she means, but, uh, we have to get out of here. "Yup. Anyway . . ." I try to hurry her along, but she doesn't seem to care that we could get into trouble. Typical Mom.

"Wow, I'm hopeless, aren't I? Maybe I'll see you tomorrow, Haley." She smiles.

"Okay, bye . . . Jenni." There, I said it. Jenni Campbell. Soon to be Petersen. Then back to Campbell. *Sigh.*

As I scuttle off my way and watch her walk in her direction, something inside me twists. I know she will meet the boy of her dreams. She'll fall in love with him. They'll get married and have me. But for some reason—reasons that don't make sense—things won't work out between them.

So maybe . . .

I shouldn't try so hard to get home yet. Maybe I should take advantage of this rare opportunity and tweak things however I have to. So that it won't happen. So that my parents won't have to go through that sadness, and neither will I. *Then* I'll come back here and try forcing an episode again.

There's one reason to postpone my leaving.

Way up ahead, as Jenni-Mom turns left down the marina path, I see Jason behind her to my right. He's arriving in his cart, parking, and walking into the Settlement Trading Post. Make that two reasons.

eleven

It doesn't look like Jake is coming after me. He might've listened to my plea and told the security guards that it was nothing. Or he might be swimming in the lagoon searching for his walkie-talkie.

The Settlement Trading Post is a grocery and souvenir shop. I look around for Jason but don't see him anymore. Inside, I find another T-shirt to wear, a solid green one with Chip and Dale over the pocket. I like it better than his mom's shirt. Checking out what other girls are wearing, I also get a pair of long blue shorts with an elastic waistband that looks like something Anma would wear, but I'm not sure I can bring myself to put them on.

As I'm pulling out the fifty Jason gave me, I notice something—my phone is missing. Great. On top of *everything else*, I lose my phone. Where did I leave it? Suddenly, the horror hits me that I left it at the top of the Whoop 'n' Holler slide. It must've slid out of my pocket when Jake caught me. I can't even go back to get it. Ugh! I'm not worried about them turning it on. There's no iPhone charger in 1982, but my pics . . . I took pics!

"You okay?" the cashier asks. Her feathered hair looks like it might crack if I tap on it, from all the shellac hair spray.

"Yeah, I just lost my phone," I tell her. Stupidly, I realize.

"Your phone number, you mean? To the trailer?"

"Nothing, don't worry about it." I hand her the fifty, and she gives me back a ten and a five, while some coins come rolling out of her machine into a little tray. I actually have change?

"Ooh, these are pretty trendy," she says, folding up the pair of shorts. "Perfect for replacing your broken ones." She smiles a sweet, grandma smile.

I'm too annoyed about my phone and hunger to be bothered by her comment right now. "How much for the Snickers?"

"Fifty cents, plus tax," she says. "Do I ring one up?"

Bargain! "Two, please." I would never, in a million years, have a Snickers bar at home. Coach would kill me. But I don't see anything healthier, and at least this has protein in the peanuts. "Thank you." I take my Disney World bag, rip open a candy bar, and head out the wooden doors.

I follow the bathroom sign around a soft-serve ice-cream stand that I don't remember being there in the future and change my clothes inside a stall. I can't do the shorts. I just can't. I leave my shipwreck shorts on but put on my Chip and Dale shirt. I put his mom's back in the tote bag and head outside.

I stroll down to the marina, veering off under the pines, still reeling from the Jenni-Mom sighting. The night is alive with the sounds of crickets and kids laughing.

"Man, I'm too late." I hear a voice next to me. When I turn, I see Jason standing there, looking fresh and showered and in a Journey concert shirt. Hey, isn't that the "Don't Stop Believin'" band? I'm totally impressed with my vintage music knowledge and, okay, *Glee* watching! He's holding a brown paper bag in his hands. "I thought you might be hungry. Brought you something to eat."

"Oh my God!" He looks so HOT! And I am very, *very* happy to see that food! I throw my arms around him in complete relief. Jason does not try to pry me off. In fact, he just laughs, and I feel his hand lightly wrap around my waist. *Nice!* "What'd you get me?"

"Some barbecue chicken and a sloppy joe. If you don't like either, I can get you something else at the tavern."

"No," I say, opening the bag and ripping into a chicken drumstick. "This is perfect."

He smiles. "A girl with a hearty appetite. I like it. Want to go sit?"

I nod, knowing I look like a troglodyte, not even able to answer with my mouth full of chicken, and, boy, do I know how to charm a man on a first date. *Is* this a date? We walk together to the edge of the water, me glancing around for any sign of Jake and the Mickey Police.

"Have you seen your dad?" Jason asks. I notice he's wearing longer shorts now, like basketball shorts. "Are these more to your liking?" he says when he sees me eyeing them.

"Yes, those shorts are great, and no, I haven't seen my dad." Not since yesterday afternoon. But I have seen my mom!

He presses his lips together and nods. I wonder if he really wants me to reunite with my imaginary family or if he secretly hopes I won't find them. "Hey, I thought maybe we could go do something fun after you're done eating. Want to?"

"Like what?" I gnaw at the drumstick.

"I'm not going to tell you. That would ruin the surprise." He flashes a gorgeous smile at me. If he keeps up with the hotness, I'll be forced to kiss him later.

"I didn't know there would be a surprise, but yeah. Can I finish my food first?"

"Sure, you just . . ." He hesitates, as if wanting to touch my mouth, but not quite. "You got some sauce. Right . . . there." He points to a spot at the corner of my lips. I know he's noticing the sauce, but I can't take my eyes off his fresh, clean-cut beachiness closing in on me.

He retreats a bit. "What? Is something wrong?"

"Nothing, you looked like someone I knew for a moment," I lie.

He smirks. "Wait, let me guess. Christopher Atkins? Girls always tell me I look like I could be his twin."

"I . . ." have no clue who Christopher Atkins is. It's times like these that I want to whip out my phone and Google Christopher Atkins on the spot. But I can't keep acting so clueless, so I just say, "Yeah, you sort of do."

"I knew it. It's the nose. Maybe I should quit my towel-shack job and be an actor. It's great that you know who Christopher Atkins is. That says a lot about you." His eyes do that thing where they disappear into a squinty smile.

"Of course I know! I'm not a moron!" *Crap, I'm such a moron.* "Don't change your look, though. You wouldn't have that Calvin Klein model, all-American thing happening, which I think suits you."

"A what model? What is that?"

"Oh, Calvin Klein? A designer brand. Never mind."

"See, I don't know much about clothes."

"Ahh, so you *admit* to not understanding the fashionable properties of my shipwreck shorts!" I point a finger at him. "Ha! Which are called Daisy Dukes, by the way."

"Ooh, Daisy Duke. Man, she can jump in my General Lee anytime," he murmurs, and I have no idea what any of that means. Then he adds, "Hey, have you ever heard of Duran Duran? They're this band from the UK. They played a song last month on that TV show *Dancin' On Air*? But I haven't heard it since, and I'm trying to remember what it's called."

Duran Duran? Aren't they those guys with the song where the girl hiccup-laughs at the beginning? I played it on Rock Band 2. I start humming it quietly.

"Yes! That one!" Jason's eyes fly open and he joins in. He actually sings pretty good! But he doesn't know the words any better than I do, because he mumbles half of them, and the other half don't make any sense. "Seen in the subway, up is a wire . . ."

"Doo-doo-doo-do-do, doo-do-do, doo-do-do, doo-doop-doo-doooooo!" We sing together, finally sharing some pop culture thing that we both understand. "I'm hungry like the wooollllf . . ." We finish off, laughing like two idiots.

"'Hungry Like the Wolf.' That's it!" he cries, sitting back, staring at me in awe. "I can't believe you knew that. Nobody I've asked has known what the hell I'm talking about."

"Well, yeah, I like that song," I say, as if everybody knows it. Doesn't everyone? Maybe they're not super famous yet. Either way, I love the way his whole face changed just now after singing and laughing so hard. His eyes and smile loosen up. Even his nose, which is strong and makes me think of running my fingertip down the length of it.

He nods. "Yeah, me too. They have a video on MTV that's sexy. That one's called 'Girls on Film.' I hope they make it big here. Have you seen that one?"

"I think so," I say, trying to remember if I ever saw it on *I Love the 80's.*

"You would remember it. It was a bunch of girls mud wrestling."

"Oh, right!" I fake-remember.

"You've seen it!" He's amazed again by me. I feel so fake. "That one is supposedly censored unless you have ONTV. You have ONTV?"

"On what?"

"Cable television. You pay for it. Not like ABC or NBC. Wow, I thought everyone had heard of cable by now."

"Well, I do. I mean, of course I know about cable. I just never heard of ONTV." I feel the urge to tell him how between my two parents' houses, I must have at least seven hundred satellite channels, more than he would even know what to do with. Jason would love hearing about it, especially since he's so into previewing things before they come out. It saddens me that I can't share that with him.

"What are you thinking about right now?" he asks quietly.

"I'm just . . ." It's going to be really hard having any kind of friendship with him if I don't come clean. Not that I'm going to. I can't. "Have you ever watched *Doctor Who*?"

His eyes get big all of a sudden. "On PBS? Yeah. You watch *Doctor Who*?" More and more, he seems impressed with things I know, as if girls don't watch sci-fi or know anything about technology or music.

"Who doesn't know what a TARDIS is?" I ask, impressing him into stunned silence. "But, I guess I'm curious to know, since you like technology, the future, and, well, EPCOT—"

"EPCOT Center," he corrects.

"Sorry, EPCOT Center. Do you think that's possible? You know, for people to travel between times like that, the way the Doctor does on the show?"

He shrugs and looks out at the lake. He obviously doesn't realize how his answer will map out the course of how much I might venture to tell him. "I think it's cool to think about it, to imagine that it might happen. But I never heard of any documented cases, so it's hard to believe." He looks at me again, judging how well I might receive his answer. "Why? Do you believe it could happen?"

I look away and start drawing a circle in the sand. Had someone asked me this two days ago, I would've said no, point blank. I've never believed much in ghosts, the supernatural, or anything that hasn't been proven, but look at everything that's happened to me! So much has changed in only two days. I'm sitting here in another time and dimension. Do I really need a scientist to validate that for me? How much more proof do I need than actual experience?

"I'm not sure," I say honestly. "I'm only now starting to think that humans don't know the tiniest fraction of what there is to learn about science. We *think* we know it all, but that's because of our egos. Things are always happening to change everything we believed just minutes before. Life is challenging that way."

I get that now, which is why Mom is always telling me not to make excuses, live my life, and never apologize, and Dad is always stressing family, family, family. Because you may never see them again.

As Jason watches the water, it seems something has changed in him. He's gone back into his serious shell. "That's smart, and yeah, you're right about that."

I touch his arm. "Hey, you okay?"

He's absorbed in his thoughts a minute more, and I feel bad for whatever I said. But then he pops up and shakes the sand off his butt, offering me a hand. "Totally fine. Ready to have a blast?"

Oh my God—a blast. I can't help but smile. I place my hand in his. It feels firm and cool. It feels really nice.

"Let's go." He leads me toward the golf carts lined up against shrubs. I couldn't be more confused about my feelings right now. Am I getting too distracted? I mean, I should be trying to find my way back to the future! The thing is, I've noticed I've been smiling. Smiling A LOT since I met Jason. That wasn't happening much before I slipped back in time. So what does it matter what year I'm in, as long as I'm finally enjoying my summer?

I have to stop obsessing over all this. First of all, there's nothing I CAN do. And second of all, if my mom and dad are both right, we should all live like there's no tomorrow. So maybe that's what I should try.

Live, as we jump into the cart and drive into the warm evening of the campground.

Live, as we sing, "Doo-doo-doo-do-do, doo-do-do, doo-do-do, doo-doop-doo-doo," driving through the wilderness roads, laughing and yelling like dorks when Jason turns off the headlights at one point.

Live, and forget, if only temporarily, that I have another life. It's the only way I will ever enjoy this moment. Because it's perfect. And if I really am dreaming, then guess what? I don't ever want to wake up.

twelve

We laugh so hard, we barely notice when we pass another golf cart and three familiar faces stare back intently. "Whoops." Jason stiffens up.

"What? What is it?" I look back, but the other cart blends into the darkness. *Oh my God, don't tell me it's Jake.*

"They're making a uey. Hold on, Haley." He steps on the gas and speeds down the road as fast as a golf cart can go. My hair flies into my face. Then I see headlights shine in our rearview mirror. "It's my brother," he mumbles.

"Shit."

"Shit is right. He's been poking around my business all day. That's why I've been avoiding him, and he's with Marsha and that Oscar dude."

My dad's in that cart too? I can't let him see me. What if he recognizes me in the future as the girl who was with Jason, the River Country towel-shack kid, thirty years ago? I'll be in so much trouble!

"We need to lose them," I tell him. I mean, this could be it. Jake will tell Jason I was trespassing in River Country, and this'll be the end of the gig.

"I couldn't agree more." Jason swerves off the road into the woods, a hard ride at twenty miles an hour. We bump and boing out of our seats like we're on WaveRunners. I screech and firmly grip the sides of my seat.

"Hang on." Jason grips the wheel, concentrating on the lit-up foliage ahead of us.

"Where are we going?" I yell, now hanging on to the frame of the cart. Behind us, his brother's headlights bounce. We'll never lose him like this. "Cut the lights," I say.

"What?"

"You know your way around, right?"

"Yeah. But so does he."

"So turn off the lights!"

Surprisingly, he chuckles. "Yes, ma'am!" He slams a pulled-out knob with the palm of his hand, and oh my friggin' God, we are speeding into absolute blackness like it's Space Mountain minus the ambient lighting. We could easily plow into a lake or canal, fall off a cliff, or who knows what! I am so stupid! This is awesome!

"Woooo!" I yell impulsively, forgetting the fact we're trying to escape unnoticed, and Jason woos with me.

We make a sharp right, and a sharp left, and then we're suddenly scraping bushes. I have to pull in my arms to keep them from getting scratched, all the while laughing. I don't know what's so funny about nearly getting sliced by branches, but the extreme retreat strikes me as hysterical.

He makes another quick turn and stops, holding his hand over my mouth. "Shh, they'll hear us. He probably turned his lights off too. Man, this is crazy." I can't see much at all of him, but my eyes work their hardest to adjust quickly. I can just make out the contour of his face. There's something extremely hot about sitting here in the dark with nineteen-year-old Jason, army-bound Jason, both of us panting like escaped convicts.

Slowly, he uncovers my mouth and checks behind us, listening carefully when I really, really wish he'd look at me instead. I've never been the kind of girl to sit around and wait for a boy to kiss me *if* I really, really wish he would, but something tells me I shouldn't be the one to make the first move. We're in 1982. This is a whole other era. What if he thinks I'm too aggressive? I don't want that. What *did* girls do in 1982?

"Do you hear anything?" he whispers.

"You, breathing." Even though it's still nearly pitch-black around us, I can hear him smile. I can feel his heat, his energy, and smell his clean skin near me.

"Sorry."

"Don't be." And I don't know why, but I take his hand and gently move it back over my mouth, then the side of my face, and lean into it a little.

"Haley . . ." His voice drops a bit.

I'm not going to kiss him. I'm just going to wait and see. In the shadows, I can now make out more of the outline of his face, his parted lips, eyes focused on my mouth. But, wow, hurry up and get it over with already. He runs his fingers down over my hair, then brings his thumb back to my mouth, sweeping it across my bottom lip. I clutch his hand and close my eyes.

"Did you hear that?" he whispers.

"No." I do not hear or sense anything outside of this bubble right now. I cling to his thick hand, breathing quietly. Then I open my eyes and glance at the only other thing I *can* truly see, the stars pulsing way up over the silhouette of big pine trees reaching up toward the velvet sky.

Jason switches back to high-alert, protective mode. He scans the thicket of trees that surround us. "That. The hissing."

I strain to listen, and yeah, I mean, I hear the sounds of mechanical things swishing through the night, but we *are* at a resort in the middle of a packed summer. It could be any car, bus, golf cart, boat, or monorail within a few miles. "Are they still following us, you think?" I ask.

"Probably. Jake would love to catch me doing anything wrong just to take the focus off of him."

Hmm, I'm something wrong? I pull my hand away from him.

He looks at me, confused. "Haley, that's not what I meant. What I mean is . . . remember that I work here. We're supposed to respect the employee-guest relationship. That's all."

"You sure?" It sounded like he'd be embarrassed to be seen with me.

He takes my hand and, looking down at it, laces his fingers through mine. "Yes. I'm sure. I just don't like my brother in my business, that's all. Okay?"

"Okay." I don't really have any reason to doubt him, but I wish he knew how I'm making a big sacrifice by being with him when I could be trying to find my way back home instead. Even though I might be stalling on purpose. To spend more time with him. Maybe.

"You hear it? Listen." He points to the cricket-chirpy area behind us.

It does sound like the flattening of grass somewhere near, along with maybe some girl giggling. "They're creeping up on us," I whisper. I sit up straight. I don't want my father to remember a girl who looked like me getting cozy with a guy in the woods.

"Yes. And we have to get out soon. The battery on this cart won't last long, especially with the extra strain we just put it under."

I'm not sure how far off the road we are, but getting even more stranded than I already am would so be the opposite of fun. "How about heading back the way we came?"

"That's what I'm thinking too." Slowly, he maneuvers his way out of our spot and drives in the direction of the road again.

I keep looking behind us. "Should we speed up?"

"I don't want to waste the battery, or we'll be walking back. Then my old man'll be pissed and won't let me use the cart anymore."

I face the front again. Any moment we'll pop through the trees and be back on the main road. Suddenly I feel Jason's hand back on my face, real soft, and I see him looking at me intently. "What?"

"I wanted to kiss you back there," he says.

My stomach does a big flip, one of those that makes you stop and savor the moment just before something awesome happens. I hold on to his hand. We're quiet for a minute. The air between us is thick with all sorts of unsaid things that are probably better that way.

All of a sudden, the glare of headlights switches on behind us, lights that were there all along, poised in the dark. "Suckers!" a guy yells, and I recognize the voice from River Country. The lights come charging toward us.

"Shit, Jake."

Shit, my dad.

"Let's go." Jason switches back on our lights and plows into the brush, annoyed as hell.

The right tire bounces over a rock. "Ahh!" I yell way out loud. "I'm so going to need a new bra after this," I mumble to myself.

Jason side-glances me with a sly smile, then he starts swerving right, left, and I get the feeling that our cart is getting weak from traversing over this rough terrain with two full bodies in it for so long. Jake, Marsha, and Oscar—*Oscar!*—have fallen behind, but they're still back there, 'cause I can see their high beams bouncing all around and hear a girl yelping.

"He's losing battery," Jason says. "That cart was last charged this morning. I know because I unplugged it right after lunch to plug mine in at River Country."

Finally, we bump over something that makes us both jump in our seats so hard, we almost hit our heads on the roof. "What was that?" I ask.

"I don't know." He slows down and backs up.

"What are you doing?"

"I wanna see." He backs up over the hard object on the ground. Behind us about fifty feet, Jake's cart lights falter. The cart lunges forward then stops, lunges again, then stops. Jason looks at his chunky, black plastic watch.

"What? Why are you looking at your watch?" *Who cares what time it is!*

On the ground, something long and dark metallic stretches into the darkness, but it's hard to tell what it is. I reach down to feel it. Smooth, cold metal . . .

HISSSSS. A loud steamy noise sends my heart racing.

"Is this what I think it is?" I say, only to be interrupted by a growing light in the distance coming around some tall trees.

"Right on time." Jason smiles. "Watch this."

"A train? There's no train in Fort Wilderness!" I yell, watching the light grow brighter, listening to the sound of metal on metal, screeching and chugging toward us.

"It's decommissioned for guests, but they still run it every so often, usually at night."

"For real?"

He smiles. "For real."

"Um, don't we need to *move*, then? We're sitting right on the tracks!" Great, I am going to die by train. Who would've thought? "Oh my God, oh my God . . ." The train is almost right on us. Its light envelops us, and the conductor blows his whistle, a real steam train whistle. "Jason, we're going to die! Move, Jason!"

Jason hugs me real tight. "I'll save you, Haley!"

"Stop it!" I smack him.

He laughs so hard and looks back at his brother, who has run toward us and is now only a few dozen feet away. At this point, I'd rather get hit by them than by the oncoming train. Marsha and Oscar-Dad are yelling out random stuff.

"Haley, relax!" Jason yells through his laughter. "You really think we'll die when we can jump out of the golf cart and run away? Holy crap, girl, you are funny as hell!"

"What?" Oh. Right. We can. Do that, I mean. Get out and run. "Well, come on, let's go. Step on the gas, Jason! What if your brother thinks we're stuck and is coming to help us?" I look back.

"We do this all the time!" And right as the train is upon us, and it looks like his brother is mere feet away, he steps on the accelerator and we push over the tracks, leaving his brother, Marsha, and Dad stuck on the other side.

"Don't look back, don't look back," Jason commands over the

sound of the passing train. "I don't want the conductor seeing it was me."

Jason drops his head on the steering wheel, but I *do* look back. An older man, older than my dad in 2014, is hanging out the engine window, yelling what is probably lots of obscenities at us as the engine passes us by. I avert my face and pretend not to hear him. The train is red, gold, green, and super, super pretty! I have never, ever seen train tracks in Fort Wilderness before, much less a real steam engine. I can't help but smile, taking in the sight. Who knows if I'll ever see it again.

"It's beautiful," I whisper.

Jason looks up. "Yes. And it's only four cars long. We have to hurry." He drives a few feet more, and I recognize the wooden lampposts of the campground signaling that we've reached the main road again.

"I can't believe we just did that. That was crazy, Jason."

"That was nothing." He looks back again, and when I follow his gaze, the last car of the train is moving past, revealing his brother, Marsha, and my dad on the other side, out of battery, pushing their cart over the tracks. Jake looks at us and offers a nice flip of his middle finger.

thirteen

The sounds of the Pioneer Hall crowds die away behind us, and we head into the darkness, winding through the tall pines. Every so often we whisk by clumps of people walking in the opposite direction, carrying folding chairs or tugging little kids by the hand.

"Where are they going?" I ask.

"Probably to watch the fireworks." Jason makes a few turns, and minutes later we arrive at the Meadow Trading Post. *Hey! This is where I met Dina, Rudy, and Marcus, next to the campfire!* It wasn't long ago, but it feels like another lifetime. I guess it was.

He parks the cart and we sit there for a moment, looking at each other. Now I'm here with Jason. Amazing how life can change in an instant. Is he going to kiss me? I've known him only two days, but I've never gotten to know anyone as quickly as I've gotten to know him. The way I'm starting to feel about him is making me nervous. As if sensing this, Jason gives me a sweet but sad smile. Then he gets out of the cart and plugs it in to an outlet.

"Let's go." Tentatively, he holds out his hand. I glance at it a moment before taking it. We walk past the trading post to a wide canal.

"Where to now?" I ask.

"You'll see. Jake won't find us here, so don't worry."

I wasn't really worried about Jake. I was worried about getting too distracted from my ultimate goal. A woody mustiness fills my senses. Must be the water. A long line of people stand around while a cast member dressed as a cowboy goes over directions. "We'll hand you your paddle, and you'll climb right in, folks, one at a time."

"Paddles?" I try catching a glimpse of the water. "They're going canoeing? At almost nine o'clock at night?"

"Yeah, the Marshmallow Marsh. That's Cowboy Bob."

The Marshmallow Marsh. Wow! I remember my dad mentioning this, too! I never paid much attention to what he was saying, but I think he said it was a canoe trip to the beach where a campfire awaits. "We're getting into boats with a bunch of people?"

"Well, no. I'm going to see if Pete is working tonight. He'll give us our own canoe. Wait here." He walks off in the direction of a rental shack, and it's the first time I really get to notice him from behind.

Very nice, my friend.

Even better than my catcher Nate back home.

While Jason is gone, I take in what everybody's doing behind me. No one has a phone in their hand. Kind of like when I go to Ranch Camp, and they make everybody check their phones in when we get there. So people are just talking to one another, paying attention to Cowboy Bob, or taking pictures with old cameras.

Fragments of conversation hit me from different angles. A lady walking by with her daughter scolds, ". . . Because your father said no. Ask again, and I'm going to skin your hide." And a man with his wife says, "Well, dear, I know that, but if we don't hurry, we'll never make it to see Fantasy in the Sky, and I did not spend three bundles only to miss the fireworks." And another one I don't even understand: "I tried to tell him that, so we'll see how he handles it at Christmas bonus time."

Christmas bonus time? Never heard of that.

The stuff they talk about seems the same as in the future. But there's something about *how* they say it. Maybe it's me, but I get the sense that everyone was just happier, calmer, and less stressed now than in the future. Is happier.

Jason comes back with two yellow oars in one hand and a lit silver lantern in the other. He holds out the oars for me to take one. "He's giving us our own boat. It's over here."

I hope Jason knows how to maneuver a canoe. I've never ridden in one before. I take an oar from him. "You sure you don't want to ride with the others?"

"We could, but we'd be with eight other people, and you'd have to listen to Cowboy Bob sing 'She'll Be Coming 'Round the Mountain' and a bunch of Disney tunes. This way, we can *talk*." He smiles.

Some things never change. Like the way guys are always trying to get girls alone every chance they get. I smile back. "Sounds good to me." He leads me to a canoe tied to the edge of a different dock. It's not standard red fiberglass. It's brown with a hand-painted Native American–looking pattern on it. Really pretty. Carefully, he gets in, sets up the lantern on the bench next to him, and holds out his hand for me. I grab it. He holds me by the wrist, steadying me down.

"Got it?" he asks, waving at Cowboy Bob, who waves back.

"Yeah. You guys know each other?"

"Bob? Bob is awesome. The whole trip is a lot of fun. You'll see."

"What about life jackets?" I ask, slapping a mosquito at my leg.

"You expecting to sink?"

"Um, no, but . . . isn't it, like, regulations or something that we wear them?"

He looks at me strangely. "If we fall in, we just swim to the edge of the creek. This isn't the *Titanic*." He chuckles and places the ends of his oars in the water. "It'd be radical if they found that ship one day."

Wow. I open my mouth to correct him, but what do I say? That the *Titanic* has been found for a long time now? I can't imagine living life not knowing something like that.

"Nothing to be scared of, except maybe some alligators in the creek."

"Alligators?"

He laughs. "Got you. Put your oar in."

I glance back at the group of four canoes being led by Cowboy Bob. "Stroke! Stroke!" Bob cries out, but some of the canoes are having trouble staying straight.

"Let's get into a rhythm and go off on our own," Jason says. "Follow me. Ready? Stroke. . . ." I push my oar through the water. "Stroke . . . stroke. . . ."

I match his movements stroke for stroke, and we are off. Into the dark canal system of Fort Wilderness with absolutely nothing to light our path but the oil lantern creating moving shadows on either side of the canal. After a few minutes it's clear that we are ahead of the pack. The buzzing and singing of the Marshmallow Marsh group fade into the distance.

Jason and I don't speak. We wouldn't dream of it. There're a million stars in the sky, the crickets are singing classic tunes of their own, and there're even flitting shadows of raccoons or some other animal on the banks of the canal. The only other sounds are of the water, sloshed by our oars, and the occasional slap of a fish on the water's surface. I feel like Pocahontas on a date with Captain Smith, painting with all the colors of the wind.

A couple of bugs flit about, their glowing green eyes like aliens'. I've seen them only a few times before. One lands in our boat. It clicks around, trying to flip over. "Lightning bug," Jason says, and bends down to pick it up.

I lean over to peer at it, but I don't touch it. "Aren't those click beetles?"

"Yeah, same thing. They're harmless." It walks around on

Jason's hand, the bioluminescent spots that look like green, glowing eyes getting bright, brighter, then dimming to dark. "My old neighbor in Kissimmee was this Cuban lady," he says. "She called them *cocuyos*. Said they were good luck." He reaches over and takes my hand. The beetle walks from his hand to mine. "Here, so you'll have good luck."

"Oh, crap," I laugh nervously. There's a beetle walking on my hand. I don't care how cool it looks with its bright lime eyes . . . it's a *beetle*. But I don't want to appear girly scared, so I let it walk up my arm for a bit before I shriek, and it finally takes off into the night.

Jason laughs. "You don't seem the scared type."

"I'm usually not."

"But you just screamed like a chicken. The girl who passed out in River Country, got up, and kept going shrieks when she sees a little bug." He laughs to himself quietly.

"I didn't pass out. I was diagnosed with epilepsy. Even though I'd only had one seizure in my life before yesterday, I sort of feel like I'm wearing a big scarlet letter *S*."

And if I ever want to get back to the future, I might have to bring on one more.

"Yeah, about that . . ." All smiles fade from his face. "Shouldn't you be finding your dad soon? How long are you going to be on your own, Haley? I mean, don't get me wrong, I like spending time with you, but your dad's going to worry, isn't he?"

I stop rowing. Jason continues without me. I watch the black shadows of the trees on the dark water. He's right; I should go back. I'm just not sure I want to anymore. "What if I stay?"

He stops rowing too, and the boat glides silently along the canal. "What do you mean?"

I shrug. "I mean, what if I want to stay here forever?" I try to give the question a more hypothetical feel.

His eyebrows draw together. "You can't do that, Haley. Think. Your dad, your family . . . Why would you even say that?"

"I'm not saying I'm *going* to. But what if?"

He blows out a relieved breath and resumes rowing, seemingly glad it was only me dreaming out loud and not a real dilemma to be dealt with. "Then we live here forever." He smiles. "You and me. We work at River Country. You could be a waitress."

"A waitress?" I scoff. "What if I want to be a lifeguard?"

"Fine, a lifeguard! You can be whatever you want, tough girl." He laughs. "We're turning now, so just paddle on one side. Your left one."

I do as he says, and the canoe turns slowly and continues along the curve of the canal. I hear the laughing of families in the distance, enjoying the evening air, and the crackling of a campfire nearby. I spy people on land sitting on folding chairs and picnic benches, as we glide by in stealth mode. How do I explain to Jason that I might not be able to return to my family? That the hypothetical question of staying here forever might be a reality for me?

It hurts to think that I can't. It'll ruin everything. Before I can say anything, he changes the subject. "What do you do when you're not wandering around campgrounds by yourself? What do you do at home? You into fashion magazines? Music?"

I laugh. "Uh, music, sure. Fashion, not exactly."

"I guess that was a stupid question."

"No. I'm just not that kind of girl, I guess. I play baseball."

I register the changed expression on his face. He looks confused now. "You mean softball."

"No. I mean baseball. I pitch for my high school team."

"Of girls?"

"Of boys. I'm the only girl on the team."

He scoffs. "Yeah, okay, and I'm a monkey's uncle."

I realize how stupid this must sound to him, since even in the future, it's hard for most high schools to allow girls in traditional boy sports, but it's too late. I already put it out there. I really want to tell Jason the truth about me. I mean, how long can I go around pretending I'm something that I'm not? "Let's just say my school is real avant-garde, ahead of its time."

"I know what avant-garde means, Miss Haley-Haley," he says, taking long, thoughtful strokes of his oar. "I'm not stupid."

What? My eyebrows crinkle together. "I never said you were stupid, Jason-Jason. In fact, I think quite the opposite."

"How do you figure?"

"Well, first off, you're a smart guy. You know a lot about technology, computers, EPCOT, movies. Second of all, you seem responsible, and honestly? Well, here's what I think. I think you should apply to colleges instead of the army."

He gets kind of quiet. Does he really think he's not college material? He could be anything. A computer programmer. An engineer that doubles as a surfer model. Maybe he's scared it'll be too hard for him? They must have some community colleges in Orlando that he could attend.

"You think so?" he asks.

I nod. "Yes."

"And you seem wise beyond your years," he says. "Don't let anybody ever change that about you."

I guess I would seem that way to him, though I don't feel that way. The truth is I have no idea what I want to do with my life either, so I don't see what right I have insisting that he go to college.

"Hey, speaking of technology, movies, and Disney," he says as his whole face lights up. "Do you think you'll still be around next week? There's a cool movie coming out. I'd love to take you to see it. Maybe you've seen the previews. It's called *Tron?*"

It's getting difficult to keep track of stuff going on in both his era and mine. I feel like I'm going to have to choose one soon and stay in it. "When does it come out?" I ask.

"The ninth, I think. I'll drive to Jupiter if you want to see it. If they're playing it over there."

Wow, he would drive two hours just to take me to a movie? How can I let him down after that? "I . . . I'd love to, Jason. I think that'd be really nice." I smile at him sadly. Because it'll probably never happen. Even if I can't find my way back home, what are the chances I'll live in Jupiter by myself?

The canoe stops moving, and Jason leans forward. He reaches out his hand and slides it into my hair, holding the back of my head. I hold my breath. A moment from now everything will change. A moment from now I'll be better than every girl who has wanted to kiss Jason this summer without luck.

"I'm glad I met you," he says.

My hand grabs his, and I lean into him. "Me too." I close my eyes.

Then there's an electricity between us as Jason gently pulls my face toward his and kisses me. Softly but wanting. Wanting but sweet, full of need and other things I don't even know how to describe. I can tell that he's done a lot more than this. How I know that, I don't know. I just do. And thinking about him having experience is making me dizzy. Because even though I've always been in control of how much boyness I want in my life, how far to let one in, what I want and what I don't want—I am nothing but a big lump of useless girl mush right now.

All I know is that I want to smile and cry at the same time. I don't want to snap out of this dream and find him gone. I don't want to tell him the truth and upset everything he's ever known either.

He pulls back and smiles that gorgeous smile, and for once I have no words. All I have are weak legs, a heart that won't stop pounding in my chest, and the memory of this beautiful canoe ride emblazoned on my mind for the rest of my life.

"That was nice."

"Yes, it was." I smile. I don't know what's happening to me.

But I can say this: My dad was not kidding about the Marshmallow Marsh. When we arrive at the beach, we carefully climb out of the canoe into a secluded area of the beach on Bay Lake that has a bonfire burning just for us. And because our canoe arrives first, we're the first ones to appreciate it.

Out on Bay Lake, there's a sparkly colored electrical water parade crossing the water. Boats carrying blue and green fish, a sea serpent, and a big American flag cruise by slowly. It's so simple and so pretty. Down the beach, families stand around watching it, reveling in its beauty.

Jason sets down our oars, grabs the lantern and my hand, and leads me to the campfire. "They'll be here any minute." He locates two boxes sitting by the campfire and opens one of them. It's filled with bags of Jet-Puffed Marshmallows, one of which he rips open. He skewers a marshmallow with a stick from another box next to it and hands it to me.

"Thanks," I say, sitting on one of the log benches that surround the campfire. "Too bad we don't have chocolate and graham crackers."

"True. But I like this better." He preps himself a marshmallow on a stick and sits next to me. "More like the old days." We roast marshmallows, and I notice a few pairs of eyes in the brush near us, raccoons waiting for a handout. I pull back my marshmallow, and as usual I've scorched the crap out of it.

Jason pulls his in, takes it off the skewer, and holds out a perfect, lightly toasted marshmallow for me. "Here, take mine." I take a bite. The smooth meltiness dissolves on my tongue, and I feed him the other half.

Soon the rest of the Marshmallow Marsh crew arrives, and we elude them by moving to the water's edge. We settle down in the sand, and I rest my head against Jason's shoulder. His gold chain reflects the firelight.

"What?" he asks.

"Nothing. This." I tug on the chain and giggle.

"My chain? Why's that funny?"

"I don't know. It just is. I don't know any guys who wear chains."

"You must not know a lot of guys." He laughs and leans his head on mine.

"*Pff*, dork." I can't explain that most guys don't wear them anymore.

But besides the bittersweet confliction, there is nothing in the world like this. Being with Jason, doing whatever we want to do, going wherever we want to go. Especially when he leans into me and kisses me again, and again, and it's the sweetest, most delicious kiss ever. I don't want this night to end. Ever.

A few minutes later a booming noise comes from the direction of the Magic Kingdom, past the Contemporary Resort, and the sky fills with sparkly fireworks. *No way. Really?* Jason looks at me to see my reaction. He sees I'm smiling and seems pleased that he planned this all so perfectly. "Mucho points for you, my friend, Mr. Disney Insider."

"Hey, working here has its perks," he says, putting his arm around me.

As much as it sucks to admit this, my dad had it right. I'm having *a ton of fun*—a *blast* even—one that I know for a fact I never would've had at Ranch Camp. He would revel in victory if he could hear what I'm thinking now—because Fort Wilderness is the best.

fourteen

When I awake, it's to the sound of the Magic Kingdom launch's trumpetlike horn in the distance. I open my eyes. *Whoa, we slept here all night?* I'm still on the beach, head cradled in Jason's arm, his hand against my side. The sun is slowly but surely heating up the sand. A few feet away is a white egret staring at us, wondering what we're doing on its turf.

Aside from the mournful horn, the morning is calm and peaceful. Amazing how soundly you can sleep when there're no texts, posts, or updates waking you up. 'Cause right now, I really don't care what anyone else is doing.

I wish we could stay here forever.

But.

I can't.

Should I be letting myself fall for a boy I can't possibly have a future with? *No, no, no.*

Seriously, what are my options? Staying in 1982 with Jason, getting married, then having a child who meets me again thirty years from now? So there'll be two Haleys, one seventeen, one about fifty? Well, no, I wouldn't exist in 2014 anymore if I disappeared from there, would I?

So if I exist here and now in 1982, does that mean my parents are *not, in fact,* missing me right now? Does that mean I could stay here, guilt-free, knowing that they're okay?

Because *this is heaven.*

I have to think about this some more.

But suddenly Jason's arm throws my head aside, and he looks at his Casio watch. "Holy shit, I'm late," he blurts, jumping to his feet. "I'm *so* late for work!" I lift myself up, resting on my elbows while he scuttles around, collecting our stuff—the oars, the bag of marshmallows, the lantern. He looks so cute and sexy when he's flustered.

"Come on, Haley, we gotta move. I can get you into River Country if you don't have anywhere else to go." *Pff.* I don't really need anyone's help getting inside River Country. I could write a book by now on how to do it.

"I don't have a bathing suit," I groan. "It's, uh, back with my dad." As much as I want to hang around and stretch this dream as long as it will go, I have to go back. Plus, it's feeling really crappy lying to him. Even if I won't have a future with him, I care for him now. He's stuck his neck out for me a couple of times already. The truth is the least he deserves.

"Yes, I noticed. Come on. We'll figure it out as we go." He heads through the trees down a nature trail I couldn't see last night.

"What about the canoe?" I ask.

"Do you see one?"

I look back at the canal. Actually, no. I wonder where it disappeared to. "I guess we're walking, then." We emerge out of the nature trail onto one of the paved loop roads where the trailers are. "Wait, I thought we were going to River Country."

He pulls me by the hand. "I need my uniform first. I'll see if I can get you a bathing suit."

"Whose? Your mom's again?" I ask. "No, that's just weird."

"I guess you're right. Fine, I'll give you some extra cash. I'm sure they have bathing suits at the Settlement Trading Post. I'll bet your dad didn't expect for you to find a rich fellow who would buy your survival here, huh?" He laughs nervously, breaking into a jog. "That's kind of cheating."

"There's a rich guy here?" I chide, glancing around.

He looks at me, mockingly wounded. "Maybe one day. I know a thing or two, Haley. I know movies, know electronics. Hey, I would've gotten a job at Radio Shack if I had a car. So, yeah, you might've met a future rich guy." He smiles, fishing in his pocket and giving me what seems to be the rest of his cash.

"I believe you," I tell him. "I think you can do anything you put your mind to, Jason. I can see you doing big things. I'll pay you back, by the way. I don't know when, but . . . I will."

We come upon a street lined with trailers, and he slows down. He turns to face me. "It's amazing how you believe in me. I want you to know I really appreciate that. Keep the money. I don't need it for anything."

I look at it a moment, then put it in my pocket. "Thanks. Of course I do."

"I just wanted you to know it." He glances down the street.

"Which one's yours?"

He points. "The one down there, the tan trailer with the brown stripes on it. You know how to get to River Country from here?"

What, he's leaving me? Well, I suppose he can't just show up at his trailer with his parents there and everything, tugging the lost Fort Wilderness girl by the hand. "Um, yeah, I'll find it. Don't worry."

He takes my face in both hands and kisses me softly, rubbing his thumb along my bottom lip. Butterflies flutter in my belly. "Go to the ticket counter and ask for a courtesy pass. I'll leave one in my name. If you see my brother, tell him I'm on my way."

His brother. *Shit, his brother!* If I see his brother, I am definitely running in the opposite direction. "See you over there," I say.

I take off to find my way to the trading post and buy myself a carton of milk and a small box of Frosted Flakes. Then I rummage through the clothes rack. I don't really see any cute bikinis, except a rainbow-striped one. I grab it to try on. I suppose if I'm going to River Country, I can't quite walk around in shorts and a T-shirt like I did last time. Jake would spot me again in a heartbeat.

Whoa. I stop sliding hangers on a rack and pull out an interesting one-piece bathing suit. It's a white-and-black diagonally striped monokini with cutouts on the sides and white plastic rings at the hips. Very retro. Very ooh-la-la. Now *this* I can see myself in. And it's size four! "Where's the fitting room?" I ask a store employee dressed as a pioneer woman.

"You can try them on right back there." She points to a curtained recess in the back.

"Thanks." I head over, slip into one of two stalls, and close the curtains. Changing in a general store makes me a little nervous. I can hear girls talking in the stall next to me.

"I know he is," one of them says. "That's why I don't think he'll even notice me."

"You have to stand out, make him look at you. I think that outfit is perfect."

"Really?"

It's my mom and Lizzie. I would recognize the rhythm of those voices together anywhere. Who are they talking about? I peek out of my curtain to find Lizzie opening theirs to step back and take a good look at my mom. "For sure. You can wear that one tonight."

I clear my throat and interrupt. "What's tonight?"

Lizzie's head whips at me in shock. My mom's pokes through the curtain. "Oh, Haley. What are you doing here?"

I twiddle my fingers at them. "Just looking for a bathing suit. You guys?"

Lizzie makes a silly face at my mom. "Well, Jenni here needs to find something to make Oscar-poo notice her."

My mother slaps Lizzie's arm. "Stop. It's Oscar, not Oscar-poo."

"Can I see?" I ask, and my mom and Lizzie exchange cautious looks. "Come on, I promise I won't laugh. Besides, I'm sure you look great."

My mom looks hesitant, but after a moment she steps out from behind the curtain. What she's got on makes me want to vomit. Long white jean shorts to her knees and a pink top with ruffles that looks like a birthday cake for a five-year-old. "Wow!" I chew on my thumbnail.

"Is that a good wow or a bad wow?" Lizzie asks.

Jenni-Mom's eyes scan my face. "It's a bad wow." Her shoulders slump as she checks herself in the mirror.

Dad said that he never felt love at first sight with my mom. That their friendship sort of evolved into love. Maybe that was the other problem, besides me. Thing is, there's not a lot to choose from as far as clothes are concerned here in the trading post. And if she wants to get an edge on Marsha, Red Bikini Girl that she is, she's going to have to step up her game.

I have to sacrifice my finding. For her.

"That's cute," I say. "Really cute. But uh . . . do you want cute?" I reach into my stall, pull the black-and-white monokini off the hanger, and push it ahead of me. "Or do you want smokin'!"

"Oohhh," my mom and Liz say in unison, their wide eyes fixed on my prize.

Mom reaches forward and takes the monokini from me. "How did I miss this? Is this a one-piece or a bikini?"

"It's both. Try it on. You look about the same size as me." I smile at her amazed expression both because of the super-cute bathing suit and my sacrificing it.

"Thanks, Haley!"

"You're welcome."

Lizzie checks the price on the bathing suit and gasps. "Forty-five dollars? Jenni, you don't have forty-five dollars on you. It's nice but not *that* nice."

"Who says we have to pay for it?" Jenni-Mom mumbles.

"Oh." Lizzie checks to see if the store employees are listening in.

I pretend to be super enthralled with the changing-room curtain. And there she is—my wild-child mom. Should I pretend I didn't hear her, or try to sway her shoplifting decision in the hopes she won't turn into the rebel my dad divorced thirty years later?

"Anyway," she says, cutting me off before I can say anything. "I'll be in the park most of the day, but I'll definitely wear this tonight. Why don't you come, Haley? There's going to be a bonfire on the beach. Everybody's talking about it."

"That sounds fun. I'll come by. Oh, and hey . . . that, with some red lipstick, and you'll get him." I wink at her. I watch my mother and cousin, excited over this new turn of events, retreat into the stall, and I hear their uplifting giggles.

The rainbow bikini fits me fine, so I head to the cashier to actually *pay* for mine, then leave the store smiling. For once I exercised some control over my parents.

Come on, Dad, I started it off. Don't let me down now.

Getting into River Country legitimately was nerve-racking at first. I was afraid to approach the ticket counter for fear that a security guard would be there waiting for me, but after giving them Jason's name and receiving my courtesy pass, it was a breeze.

I find a shady spot under the pine trees, away from the lagoon pool where Jake is working, but also close to the entrance in case I need to make a run for it. I wriggle out of my shorts and shirt and lie out on a lounge chair with a view of Jason's rental shack, keeping my eyes peeled, like a fugitive on the lam.

Do I return to Whoop 'n' Holler? Do I try to see if the time travel will work again? Do I need my phone? I had it last time. Will it work if I don't have it? Gah. So many questions! The fact that I can't figure out how to trigger time travel bothers me to no end. I always get what I want, and this whole trip has been nothing but a giant exception to that.

I spot Jason talking to customers, looking his usual hotness. It's Saturday—I think—and this place is booming. Tomorrow is July 4. There's a line for just about everything—the zipline, the Whoop 'n' Holler slides, and to the left of that, the inner tubes.

Someone nearby has a boom box, probably the biggest boom box I've ever seen, and it's playing that song that goes, "Physical, physical, I wanna get physical. . . ." The girl listening to it is slathering on what looks like pure oil. In fact, as I look around, I don't see anything that looks like bottles of SPF lotion, just brown bottles of oil, oil, and more oil.

When I glance back around the other direction, Jason is walking toward me. "Hey there, now that's what I'm talking about." He purses his lips in approval of my bikini and leans down, hands on his knees to check me out. "Nice, Haley, nice."

"Thanks." I smile and shield my eyes from the sun.

"You going to lie here, or go ride something?"

Yes, Whoop 'n' Holler. I have to. My dad is missing me. I stare at Jason's amazing eyes one more time in case I never see them again. "I think I'll try the inner tubes." Each lie I tell him now feels like a paring knife slicing away at my decency as a human being.

"Good idea. Well, stay away from the slides this time." He touches my face. "And come see me if you get bored. Or even if you don't." He kisses me, and my stomach flips again. Ugh. How can I go? But how can I stay?

"Go. I don't think cast members should be kissing girls while on the job," I say, pushing him back gently.

"All right, I'll catch you later." He jogs off toward the rental booth. My heart breaks watching him go. I know I was ready to go home only yesterday, but after spending the night with him, now I don't know what to think. I know I want to help my parents have a moment. And I know I want to get closer to Jason. In fact, the thought makes me dizzy, especially when I replay the moments of us kissing last night, over and over in my mind.

Damn, I am so screwed.

I need to start rehearsing what I'm going to tell him. I also need to prepare for the worst—he won't believe I'm from the future and may not talk to me again. But regardless, I have to come clean. It'll go something like this: *Hey, guess what? I have something to tell you. I slipped back in time through some dimensional shift—and here I am. . . . Ta-da! And guess what? The future is RAD! Oh, and by the way, your summertime pal, Oscar? Yeah. That's my dad.*

This is gonna suck.

I close my eyes and feel the sun's warmth on my body. It's not as hot as it would normally be in the summer. Or has that changed too, global warming and all? The smell of coconut oil wafts under my nose. The shrieks of children in the background remind me of the night I stood at the iron wall with Dina and listened to what I now realize were the ghostly echoes of River Country. I felt its presence calling me.

And now I'm here.

Except . . . I didn't choose to come here. I've always believed our choices and actions form our future, so how did I end up here? I hate to think this, but could it have been fate? I can't subscribe to that. It would mean that fate was responsible for my parents' split-up and my time apart from them. That doesn't seem right. It was their actions, or inactions, that caused it. It was also me, being born and taking sides, that eventually forced them apart.

Fate had nothing to do with that. It can't *possibly* be in control. I am. I'm in control. Which means there's something I'm not doing right in my efforts to return. I need to enjoy my last responsibility-free moments in River Country and Fort Wilderness, then go try to prompt a seizure at the slides again and hope that Jake doesn't see me.

"And so we meet again."

Who always appears right when I least expect him to.

fifteen

Quickly, I gather my shorts, shirt, and flip-flops, but he grabs me by the arm. "So, what's your good reason?"

I yank my arm out of his. "For what?"

"For being here at night?" He stares at me awaiting an answer, standing there, hands on his hips, mustache twitching. "For trespassing and throwing my walkie-talkie down the slide and nearly getting me into a boatload of trouble."

Despite my nerves being on high alert, I hold down a snicker. "You gotta admit, that was pretty funny." I walk toward the main entrance in a huff, but he runs ahead, takes me by the arm again, and steers me toward a nature path where some guests are pointing and taking pictures. The nature trail! Where I climbed into River Country that fateful night.

"I think a *thank-you* is in order. You're lucky I didn't tell security exactly where you were when they asked for your location. That's why you're not sitting at the Orange County Police Department right now."

I stare at him. You know, upon closer inspection, there's something gentle hiding in his eyes. It's hard to see, but I think it's there. "You didn't tell them where I went?"

"Like I said, a thank-you is in order. Only because my brother seems to have it bad for you. Otherwise, I wouldn't have cared. Believe it or not, I have a heart. A little one."

His brother has it bad for me? I wonder if he thinks this because he saw us together in the golf cart, or because Jason told him all about our evening last night. "Thanks. I appreciate it," I say. "Now can I go?"

"Not until you tell me what you were doing in the park after closing hours. And what this is . . ." He pulls something out of his shorts pocket. My phone! The screen has a big crack across the top corner, but otherwise it's still in one piece. "Where did you get this?"

"It's just a phone, a cellular phone. And I was there because sometimes I can't control where I go. I suffer from seizures, remember?"

"You suffer from lying, I think." His stern face challenges me. Not one muscle moves. "Why were you there? And don't lie, because you tend to look to your left when you do, so I can always tell." He smiles underneath his mustache, but it's not a very nice smile, and . . . *Do I really look to my left?*

Sigh. Okay. Fine, I'll give him a clue. Just a small one, enough for him to leave me alone. "Look, I'm lost. I'm not trying to break in, steal anything, or cause trouble. I'm just looking for my way out." I *was*, anyway. "Because the thing is—"

"Out of where?" Jake asks, and I can see that he's really trying to understand.

Suddenly Jason is there between us, pulling Jake by the arm and making him turn away from me. "What do you want with her?" he says impatiently to his brother. I take the confrontation as an opportunity to slowly back away. "Haley, where were you going?"

"She's leaving. She's looking for her way out, she just told me. And get this, she says this thing is a phone."

Jason glances at the object in his brother's hand. "It *is* a phone, stupid." And then he turns to me with hurt eyes. "Is that true? You're leaving now?"

"No. He didn't let me finish. I have to explain."

"You knew that?" Jake asks, surprised.

Jason shrugs and shakes his head. "What's going on with you two? Is something wrong?"

"Little brother, you should know . . ." *No! You can't tell him. I'm telling him!* I try getting in between them and putting my hand over Jake's mouth, but his arm is too strong for me as he holds me back. "That your little girlfriend here isn't who she's pretending to be."

"I'm not pretending to be anybody," I scoff, and turn to Jason. "Whatever he says, don't believe him. I'll explain to you myself. When he's not around."

Jason's eyes are focused on me, not sure what to believe, especially after I just tried to shush his brother. "Okay . . ."

"Dude," Jake says, showing Jason my phone. "She lost this at the top of the slides last night, and you know how I know that? Because I was helping to close up after the park closed, and she was there, Jason. In the park . . . *after* hours. You figure it out, man."

Jason takes the phone from Jake. I can see the wheels in his brain working overtime as he looks at it, at his brother, and at me, trying to figure out what the hell is happening. "What were you doing there?" he asks me. "I thought you were at the trailer getting ready to come see me."

"Which trailer? *The* trailer?" Jake is beside himself with shock. "You took her *there*? Bro, I told you, you are not allowed to use that place! That is just for me and Marsha."

"Except Marsha never wants to go there with you," Jason mumbles under his breath.

"Shut up!" Jake yells. "She does; she's just taking her time."

"Yeah, okay, buddy, whatever you say," Jason says.

How does Jason know this? Does he talk to Marsha? Are they close? A pang of jealousy hits me suddenly.

"You'd better watch yourself," Jake says.

"Or what? Look, the girl needed a place to stay." He turns to me. "Haley, what were you doing here at night? Be honest with me."

Before I can answer, Jake does a little hop, then brings his hand to his forehead. "Holy shit, dude. First, you let her use the trailer I told you *I* had dibs on. Then you're asking her for the truth when

I *just* gave it to you! Whose side are you on? You've known her for what, two days?"

"Shut up!" Jason turns and pushes his chest up to his brother's. "I wasn't talking to you."

"Yeah? Well, I was talking to you, dipshit."

"Go to hell." All of a sudden, Jason pushes Jake away from him hard, and now it's really on. You can tell because the people walking on the nature trail are not talking about the birds anymore. They're trying to tiptoe their way around these two without getting hurt. It's weird to see Jason so pissed off. And worse knowing it's over me.

"Guys, stop! I'll talk, but not here. We need to go somewhere else."

Jake shakes his head. "I can't go anywhere. I'm on a break. I need to get back."

I hold out my hand. "Then can I have my phone, please?"

He smiles in a way that makes me want to break his teeth. "Until you explain why you have no parents, no place to stay, why no one can explain who you are . . ." Jake counts all my offenses off on his fingertips, then snatches back my iPhone from Jason. "I'll hold on to this. I'll be back later. I expect to find you still here. And you"—he looks at Jason—"figure out a way to get this thing to turn on."

Yeah, good luck without a charger. Although, I guess if anyone could figure that out, it'd be Jason. He did say he would've worked at Radio Shack if he had a car. Wait. . . . "You can get this to turn on?" *That's it!* Once he gets it on, I'll take it back with me to Whoop 'n' Holler and try the whole forced-seizure experiment all over again, this time with a charged phone. Hopefully, the conditions will match, and I'll go home.

Jake laughs. "He hot-wired a car. I'm sure he can turn on a dead appliance."

Wait . . . huh? I stare at Jason, my mouth open. "You hot-wired a car?"

"Oh. Didn't he tell you?" Jake asks in mock surprise.

Jason looks like he could fold his brother into a pretzel right about now. "Shut. Up. Jake. And how the hell should I know how that thing works?" He shrugs, pointing at the phone.

"You're the crafty smarty-pants. You figure it out."

"I thought you said college wasn't for you," I mumble under my breath.

"I said I wasn't sure, Haley." He looks hurt that I would even mention what we talked about in private. Even more that his brother would throw him under the bus like he just did.

"Is that what he said?" Jake scoffs. "I suppose car theft on his record never came up in conversation? The only reason he even has a summer job here is because of me convincing them he needed help getting rehabilitated. And because he's a cute kid." He laughs, reaching out to condescendingly slap Jason's face.

Jason shoves his hand away. "It was one time, asshole. What's done is done."

"Take it easy, buddy," Jake says, raising his hands in mock surrender. "Let's hope, huh? I gotta get back." He walks off, his stocky body pushing forward with every step, like a robot on a mission.

Jason shakes his head and crosses his arms. I think he's going to tear into his brother again, but he just looks off into Bay Lake, not even defending himself, like it's all true, or he's just really good at containing his anger.

"You're demanding answers from me; meanwhile, you have secrets of your own?" I ask.

"It was one time, Haley, two years ago. I'd never been in trouble before." He leans back against a lamppost. "And we didn't have money, not that that's any reason. I know it was wrong."

"Is that why you won't apply to college?"

He doesn't answer.

This burns me. Here we have a smart, sweet guy, with a good head on his shoulders, but more important, with the drive to do better, and still his brother has to give him a hard time for it.

"So what?" I call out after Jake, glad to have something else to argue about besides me and my mysterious phone. "He's doing the right thing now, isn't he? He just got a slow start. Give him a break."

Jake looks back at us and points to my phone in his hand. "Figure it out."

"Dick," Jason mumbles to himself.

I agree, but I can't do this.

I can't get so involved nor care this much. I need to tell him the truth, then try my experiment again. As soon as possible. Around us, people continue about like someone released the pause button. Bad thing is, I'm left with a hurt and confused Jason. He side-glances me, eyebrows narrowed together.

"Who are you really, Haley, *if* that's your real name. Are you going to tell me what's going on?"

"Are you going to judge me?" Our gazes lock on one another. If he's not going to listen with an open mind, then I'm not talking. But, somehow, things are different. He seems to regret having helped me out, now that he knows I'm a liar with a secret. Not that he should talk.

His voice is soft, wounded, and tired. "Have I judged you yet? There's a bonfire tonight on the beach. Eight o'clock. Look for me there." And as he's walking away, I feel like my head is going to explode.

It all hits me at once.

How his brother almost blew my cover. How Jason's slightly-below-average self-esteem and juvenile record explain a lot about him. How much I've grown to care about him in so short a time. How I'm going to have to explain what's happened to me the past seventy-two hours in a way that won't confuse the crap out of him. But most important, how I may get out of 1982, and if I do, how much my life is going to suck without him.

sixteen

Walking out of the River Country restrooms, I run into Marsha coming in, red bikini, hot body, and all. "Oh, hi, Haley! Long time no see. Nice chase you gave us last night." She giggles.

"Hey, you. Yeah, that was fun. Maybe we'll do it again later?" I'm about to keep walking when I realize opportunities like these don't come every day. In fact, they will never come again. I touch her on the arm. "Hey, can I ask you something?"

She stops and flashes a polite but curious smile at me, towel dangling from the crook of her elbow. "Yeah, sure."

"If you're not into my dad—I mean, Oscar, sorry—would you tell me?"

At first she seems confused by my slip of words. Then she cocks her head slightly and puts on a look that reminds me of that Scarlett lady from *Gone with the Wind*, one of my grandma's favorite movies. "Why, Miss Haley, are you interested in Oscar?"

"Huh? Oh, no. It's not like that."

"Are you sure, because I'm almost positive you had it for Jason. Not that I blame you." She shrugs. "And he's really taken a liking to you, too." She takes a moment to scan my body from top to bottom. A little smirk appears at the corner of her lips. "Not that I blame him."

"It's not me. I have a *friend* who likes him."

At this, her eyes widen, and her playful smile spreads across her face. "Oohh, a friend. Well, if you must know, I was trying to make Jake a little jealous by flirting with Oscar. He's too controlling. I need to keep him on his toes. You know what I'm saying, don't you?"

"Uh, yeah, sure. He seems controlling." I move out of the way to let someone into the bathroom.

"He is. It's so annoying." Her voice falls flat. She stares at a spot on the bathroom wall. "I'm sure it's given poor Oscar the wrong idea, so . . . I'll make it clear to him later that we won't be more than friends. Sorry, I didn't realize."

"Oh, no, no. That's okay. I'm just trying to help my friend out." Actually, I'm hoping that between his sadness over Marsha's confession to him and my mom in her new, hot monokini, they'll get that love-at-first-sight start they really need to have.

Marsha smiles at me. "You know, you're a real sweetheart, and quite the matchmaker. I hope you win your father-daughter challenge.

I wouldn't want to say good-bye to you just yet." Her smile grows wider.

"Wait, how do you know about that?" I ask. I don't remember telling her about my dad fake-leaving me behind in Fort Wilderness. I only told that to Jason. And I'm pretty sure he's tried his best to stay away from his brother the past couple of days, so she didn't hear it from Jake.

"Why, Jason, of course. He can't stop talking about you. Haley, Haley, Haley . . . makes me want to change my name to Haley!" She laughs and walks into an empty stall. No way. Is Marsha really hot for Jason? *My* Jason? But for some reason, he hasn't been interested in her. A part of me feels sad. All those looks, but the guy she wants doesn't even notice her. But more important, she said he talks about me all the time.

Another part of me is reeling—he thinks about me as much as I think of him. This is only going to make things harder when it comes time to say good-bye.

Outside, I walk by a row of lounge chairs and see my dad lying out in the sun. He's got headphones on, and he's pretending to be reading *Muscle and Fitness* magazine. *Seriously, Dad? Ha-ha.* But I know he's on the lookout for Marsha, because he keeps glancing at the restroom door and twiddles his fingers at me when he notices me walking by.

Not only that, but next to him are Anpa and Anma, who died when I was a baby, so I don't remember her much. I slow down to take a good look at them. There they are, younger, tanned, and happy. Hardly any gray on either of them. None of them thinks twice about the girl getting a nice long stare at them as she walks by. In fact, my grandmother is reading a paperback, and Anpa is folding back the pages of a newspaper.

Wow. Look at her. So pretty. I'd only seen her in old pictures. They don't do her justice. We really don't know anything about life, do we? This is all so . . . life changing. So much, in fact, that I'm totally overwhelmed. I stop to take in all of River Country like a living old photo.

Amazing place.

And even though I really don't care for the rides at water parks, I'm here. My dad would kill me if he knew that I'd been and didn't experience it all for myself. So instead of heading back to my chair, I venture into the attractions. I wade into the lagoon and bump around my inner tube on the rapids; I even do the zipline and notice Jake watching me right before I smack the stopper and fall into the clean, green water. I make sure to stay away from the Whoop 'n' Holler, even though it looks like the most fun of them all.

I'm not sure why I stay away.

Maybe because I'm already planning to slide tonight, with my iPhone on this time, assuming Jason can get it to turn on, my attempt at re-creating the same conditions as when I fell through. Or maybe there's another reason. Maybe I'm not ready.

I stand in the lagoon, wipe the water from my eyes, and try to see Jason's rental shack from here. There he is, working. Working hard. No. I don't want to go yet. I want to see him overcome this rut of his. I want to see him get whatever it is he wants. I want to see what becomes of him.

Of us.

The bonfire on the beach is a way bigger deal than the smaller one after the Marshmallow Marsh. It's huge, with tons of people hanging out around it. First of all, this sort of thing would never be allowed in my time. An unsupervised fire near Disney guests? That is a lawsuit just waiting to happen! Second, approaching it from even way back here, I can hear the laughter and shrieks of girls that always indicate a good time. But for me, my time has arrived to come clean. My heart pounds in my chest as I approach the beach.

It's a hot and dark evening. I know this beach well, after having spent the night a hundred yards from here with Jason. The familiarity of this area of Fort Wilderness—Pioneer Hall, the Settlement Trading Post, River Country, this stretch of beach—has been a big comfort to me these past two days. The biggest comfort being Jason. Even the faces of guests I've come to see around here are like the faces of family welcoming me home.

Whether I stay in 1982 or go home, one thing is for sure—I can't live here. And I'm going to miss this place when I'm gone. It's all about to change. The innocence, my preservation of this illusion, the perfect summer night with the most perfect summer boy. In just as little as half an hour, it could all escape me, rise into the sky like the lit embers of these fires.

I take a quick inventory of who's who and recognize a few girls from River Country and a big group of teens who hang out every night, but that's it. Except a guy sitting by himself on a wooden dock post. Oscar-Dad? He looks so serious, his eyebrows so dark, so young. He looks . . . wounded.

I'm guessing Marsha talked to him. He plays with a little rock, dropping it from one hand to the other, until he finally flings it into the lake. Is my mom here? I look around but don't see her. But I do spot Jason sitting in a hammock that's tied between two palm trees. One flip-flopped foot rests on the ground, and he uses it to slowly rock himself. He watches the bonfire from back here, his thoughts lost in the flames. He went back to his trailer to shower, apparently. He's wearing a black Police T-shirt with some old-school, red digital symbols on it.

He sees me approaching in the sand and, for once, doesn't smile. "Hey," I say, hooking my thumbs through my belt loops, stopping right in front of him.

"I like your shorts," he says, mustering up some words.

I look down at my Daisy Dukes. "Thanks. I know how much you love them."

He laughs to himself, more like a hiccup than laughter. Whichever girl was screeching before starts up again, and now I see a guy pick her up and carry her to the water, pretend-threatening to dump her in.

"So what's going on, Haley?"

I take a deep breath and let it out real slow. "You promised you were going to believe me."

"I said I wouldn't judge. Which I won't." His eyes capture the firelight and movement of the people on the beach.

"This isn't easy, so bear with me." I sit on the edge of the hammock and ease myself in with him slowly, managing to get into a cross-legged position. His eyes are flat, observant, and cautious. "I know you're wondering," I begin.

He looks down as he plays with a piece of dry palm frond between his fingers. "Wondering only begins to describe."

"Well, before I say anything, I want you to know that I've really enjoyed being here with you, Jason. No matter what happens, I'll always appreciate everything you've done for me. Really, you're a good friend, and you didn't even need to be. I'll always cherish that."

He tosses the piece of palm frond onto the sand and crosses his arms. "Is this a good-bye?"

"No. At least, I hope not. But what I'm going to tell you isn't something you hear every day, so you need to be ready. As ready as you can be."

"Just spill the beans, Haley."

"Right." *One more deep breath. And . . . here goes everything.* "Jason . . ."

He waits. He pushes his chin out a bit, patiently waiting for me to find the courage.

I close my eyes. I can't control what anybody will say or think of me. I can't control anything anymore at this point. I may as well get it over with. *Just say it and see what comes.* "I'm from the future."

There.

I wait for his response but realize I'm not going to get one right away. His eyebrows draw together, and there's a sort of bemused look on his face. He's waiting for me to explain more, so I do. "I'm from the year 2014. I was staying here at Fort Wilderness when I had a seizure while on a scavenger hunt with some friends. I fell down the Whoop 'n' Holler slide, and I ended up in the water where you and your brother found me."

I don't tell him how River Country was abandoned at the time, nor anything about my parents. He watches me intently, no doubt analyzing all that I'm saying. A muscle in his cheek twitches. Still, he says nothing. *What is he thinking? He thinks I'm crazy, doesn't he?*

"Remember the little girl said she didn't know where I came from? Well, that's because I just appeared. Or how I wasn't wearing a bathing suit? That's because my shipwreck shorts are what I was wearing when I disappeared. Remember I asked you what year it was?"

He's listening. Listening, but not talking.

"Well, that's because I honestly didn't know. Everything looked so strange to me."

On the beach, some people cheer and clap, and I see that the nightly water parade is starting. Soon there will be fireworks again like last night, but it will never be the same. I'm losing Jason.

I fight back the tears. "My iPhone? The thing that your brother kept? That's a really common cell phone in the future. Like, practically everybody has one. We use them to call each other, text—which are these messages you type when you don't want to talk. We can look at weather, make lists, research on the Internet, which is probably the thing you'll find the most fascinating when you get there, Jason. You can find information on just about any topic in the world, pictures, music . . . It's pretty much the world at your fingertips." I cover my face with my hands, then flip them up in frustration. "It's like EPCOT, only way more amazing! And I've been holding all this in since I met you when I knew how much it would fascinate you."

But still . . . he says nothing.

I still don't mention my parents. I can't risk them finding out through Jason or Jake and losing their potentially big moment. Besides, I don't want to intervene in their lives anymore. It doesn't seem right. It feels like cheating.

"Jason?" My brain is going a mile a minute. I really need to hear his thoughts. I lean forward and touch his hand, but he pulls it back. "Can you say something?"

"Like what?" His words are bullets. Short and quick, but painful. He doesn't believe me. I'm hurting him, and he wants me to stop and say things that make sense. Not this crap. "I thought you were going to tell me that you were homeless. Or a runaway, or something. I don't know what I'm supposed to say to this."

"I know." I let out a sigh. "But it's true. I wouldn't lie to you."

He gives me a scolding glance.

"Okay, well, I wouldn't lie to you *anymore*. That's the reason I'm here telling you all this, because I really care about you, and I didn't want us to go on unless I was totally honest with you. So that's it."

"That's it, huh? And I'm just supposed to accept that."

"Well, not *supposed* to. But I'm hoping you will, because it's true."

"Why were you in River Country after closing hours?"

"Because I was trying to find my way home."

I can see a multitude of emotions finding their way through his eyes, his face, his tense body. "You were going to leave without saying good-bye to me?"

"I . . ." *Is that his worry?* "I wasn't sure it would work. I honestly have no idea how I got here. I was experimenting, trying to see if I would go back to my time. Or maybe I didn't want it to work, I don't know. All I know is that I set out to find a way to get back, but the more I've gotten to know you and this whole place and time, the more . . . I don't want to go home."

His eyelids blink heavily, but his silence hurts more than any words could. This is it. I need to swim over to River Country right now, like I did that night, and just pray that I get the hell out of here. I've ruined everything. Of course I did. It was bound to happen. Who would ever believe such craziness?

"You think I'm nuts, don't you?" I ask, sitting up straight. "Just tell me; I can take it."

"I don't know what to think, Haley."

"I know; I understand. Look, if you get my phone to turn on, I'll show you things you wouldn't believe. Maybe that'll help. Or ask me questions, and I'll do my best to answer them."

"Are there flying cars?"

"No, no flying cars. But we do have some that run without gas."

"Is there World War III?"

"What? No. Well, our troops are out right now in Afghanistan, but—"

"Afghanistan? What about the Soviet Union?"

"What is . . . you mean Russia? No. There's no war there."

"Nuclear warheads?"

"Nobody's using them. That I know of."

He seems relieved. "Does anything hit our planet, any asteroids . . . what about aliens?"

"No, none of that, Jason. Most everything is still the same. I mean, we know a lot more, I think, about what's in space, and we've sent out a lot of space shuttles, but I think most of the changes have been to technology. And people. People are way different. Take my mom. My mother has an envelope *full* of love notes from my dad. Yet nobody writes love letters anymore. Stuff like that."

He watches me fixedly, judging.

"It's an attitude thing. I can't explain it. It's almost like you guys all seem so innocent, but that's actually a good thing. I sort of wish my life were as pure and simple. Everything always seems so friggin' complicated, starting with my parents' divorce."

"Your parents are divorced?" He seems genuinely affected. Seriously, like the first person who actually blinks when I say that. "I am so sorry about that. That must be tough."

"It is. I think it hurt me more than I'd like to admit." I'm surprised by how close I am to crying right now. I swallow hard. I know divorce is a very common occurrence in my time, but that doesn't make it any less painful. Finally, someone isn't trying to tell me, *You'll be fine, You'll get used to it,* or *You'll have two sets of presents at Christmas.*

Jason reaches forward and takes my hand. I fight back the urge to cry. His hand feels nice in mine. Wide, boy hands.

"So you don't think I'm crazy or making this up?"

"I don't think you're making it up on purpose. I'm just wondering how your seizure might have affected your brain, your ability to reason."

"Wait, you think I'm *imagining* all this? How can I think to imagine things I've never seen before, Jason? Those arcade video games in the pizza parlor? I'd never seen those in my life! Except for maybe Pac-Man, 'cause I mean, who doesn't know Pac-Man and Ms. Pac-Man?"

His face lights up again, the way he usually does when I'm not breaking his heart. "You've played Ms. Pac-Man? It just came out! I'm dying to try it! I keep asking them over at the pizza place to get one, but they said it'll be a while. How is it? Is it good?"

"It's . . . it's great!" I say. I don't think I've ever played it, but he doesn't have to know that. Overhead, the fireworks are starting. The booms fill the night as the colorful sparkles light up the sky. As beautiful as they are, it's noisy out here. "Do you want to talk about this somewhere a little quieter?"

He shrugs. "I'm fine here. I'm waiting for my brother to get back. He went out to buy a five-volt power supply and some wire for me."

"For what?"

He watches the fireworks as if in a trance. "For hot-wiring your phone."

Oh, wow. This is going to be awesome. If it works, I'm going to have a ton of stuff to show him! We can't do it in front of people, though. It'll draw a crowd, and the last thing I need is more attention.

Suddenly, from the path leading here from the marina, I see a vision. A beautiful, sexy young girl in a white gauzy beach shirt, and underneath her see-through shirt, a shapely body highlighted by a black-and-white monokini. Her lips are cherry red, and her hair is feathered with white earrings underneath. She's an eighties dream girl, flanked by Lizzie, who I can tell is proud to be escorting her.

I'm not the only one who sees her. Half the bonfire crowd quiets down when they do, before resuming their talk again when they see she's a little on the young side.

"I know that girl," Jason says. "I've seen her around River Country. I think she spends the summer here. She's always where she shouldn't be."

I watch my brooding father until the very moment when his eyes fall on her, capture her, and follow her every movement. From the time she strides by him, giving him a light flip of her hair, to the moment when a couple of guys come up to her and Lizzie to say hi, my dad's reaction is priceless. He's a cat, watching and waiting, until she finally breaks away to sit apart with Lizzie. And that's when my dad, heart taken aback, Red Bikini Girl long forgotten, makes his move. He comes up to them and crouches in the sand.

Hi. I can see his mouth forming the words. *I'm Oscar.*

Hi, she replies. *Jenni.*

My heart feels lighter than air, and I don't think I've ever been happier than I am right now. There it is—the magic moment they were missing. No matter what happens with Jason, at least I know I might've had a hand in Mom and Dad staying together.

"Haley Petersen?"

I whip my head around, and standing there are two men I've never seen before in my life. Jason and I exchange looks.

The shorter of the two speaks again. "Would you come with us, please?"

seventeen

I never dreamed the Mickey Police could really arrest anyone. After getting escorted off the beach by these guys, who are dressed like any other guests, except for their Wilderness Explorer badges, I turn and see Jason standing there, powerless to help me. "Just go. I'll find you," he says.

Then I'm being whisked away in a truck to, I can only assume, the Fort Wilderness main offices.

"Am I in some kind of trouble?" I ask from the backseat of the pickup.

I see my captor's eyes in the rearview mirror. They remind me of my dad's in our car when I thought being taken on vacation with family was torture. When I was young and stupid, almost three forever days ago.

"That depends, Miss Petersen, on your responses to some questions."

What are they going to ask? My stomach tightens; my heart pounds. I try to relax. *It's going to be fine. Just be honest. Stay calm.* Though I don't see how honesty will get me out of this. In this case, it'll make it worse.

We wind through the roads, and I wait for their questions, but the two guys only mumble things to each other. "They ready for her?" and, "Yep, they told us to bring her in."

When we get there, they open the truck door for me, and I don't see the registration building that's there in the future. In fact, the few cars coming in pull up to ticket windows and check in right from their vehicles. Instead, there's a big trailer off to one side, which is where we are apparently headed.

I totally understand why cops flank people when they're bringing them in, because all I want to do is run away, but Officers Chip and Dale are on either side of me, ready in case I do. "Miss Petersen, do you have any belongings in your possession—keys, wallet, money?"

"No." I left the trailer key underneath the mat again when I went there to change, I have no wallet, and my only worldly possession is my phone, which Jake confiscated. "Just some change in my pocket."

"Great, would you come this way, please?" They're all smiles, probably to ease any fears I might have and not because they know the torture that awaits me. Inside, I'm taken to a small room, where two older men are waiting, both of them laughing about something totally unrelated to me, which is a relief. "Have a seat, Miss Petersen," Officer Chip says.

One of the other two men, holding a mug in his hand and wearing a beige shirt with the Fort Wilderness logo of Mickey in a coonskin cap, sees me and smiles. "Ah! Miss Petersen. Fred, coffee?"

So Fred is Chip's real name. He waves his hand and closes the door behind us. "Oh, no thanks. If I do, I won't catch one wink tonight."

The one seemingly in charge folds his hands on the desk in front of him. He's older than my dad, maybe sixty or so, gray hair at the temples and a really red face. "Miss Petersen, how are you this evening?"

"Fine, thanks. You?"

They all chuckle. "Just fine, thank you for asking," he says, still smiling. "Do you know why you're here?"

"No."

"No?" His eyes widen, bemused by my adolescent rebellion. Already! After less than a minute. "Well, Miss Petersen, I will help you. You are here because you have been wandering the campground for a few days now, though neither you nor any family members seem to be registered guests. You've been seen trespassing in the water park after hours. Several employees have described you, and you even fled our medical clinic. Some say you're from Atlanta; some say you're from Jupiter."

One of the officers chuckles. "Jupiter."

This man in charge continues. "Nurse Thomas was so very worried about you."

"I left because I wasn't feeling sick anymore."

"Oh, I can tell, I can tell. So we need to know if there is anyone at this facility that you are staying with, so that we may inform them, since you are a minor. Are you not, Miss Petersen?"

If I say I'm a minor, then I have to tell them who I'm staying with. But if I tell them I'm an adult, then I'll get arrested for trespassing on the spot. *What to do?*

"Miss Petersen?" He waits. They all wait. I don't know what to say. I feel fused to my chair. "Okay, then, do you have any identification? Anything?"

I have nothing.

"Miss Petersen? You're going to have to cooperate if you want us to help you."

Help me? If they wanted to help me, they would release me and let me try finding my way home without interfering. "I . . ." What do I do? "I had a seizure, and uh . . . when I woke up, I wasn't sure where I was nor who my family is. For all I know, I am staying with someone, but I can't remember who they are."

Yes, buy time. Excellent bullshit.

At this, his eyebrows rise in surprise. This is something he didn't expect to hear. "Well, then, if your memory seems to be the problem, then we're going to have to call in the Orange County Police. Unless there's *something else* you want to tell us. Because I'm afraid it's out of our hands at this point."

Okay, that did not work as I'd hoped.

I squirm on the edge of my seat. If I maintain this as my story, what happens next? Will I have to wait in this little room until the police arrive? Do I tell them my time-travel story? They'll call the police regardless of what I say. I'm what some like to call—*screwed*.

"I, uh . . ."

Four faces stare at me.

There's only one thing to do. The only thing I've ever known how to do, sadly. Manipulate—charm—control. God, I am a terrible human being. But I need to. "Did you know that the *Titanic* is recovered just a few years from now?" Their faces all soften into confusion, and they exchange looks. "By a crew of sea explorers. It's sitting two miles down at the bottom of the North Atlantic in two huge pieces."

"I beg your—"

"And did you know that in 2001, there's going to be an attack on the World Trade Center, and the twin towers are going to fall?"

"Two thousand one? What kind of nonsense is she talking?" says Officer Fred to the room before frowning at me. "What are you saying?"

"I'm telling you about the future."

"That's it. Get Orange County on the line, will you?" insists the guy in charge.

"Just listen." I interrupt with a hand. "And did you know that EPCOT is going to be a huge success, mostly because of the country pavilions and Food and Wine Festival, and a fast ride called Test Track?"

"How do you know about these things?" In-Charge demands,

turning to the other guy who was drinking coffee with him before I arrived, but he just shrugs. "Find out who she's been talking to, would you?"

I go on. "And that *Tron* is going to become a cult classic, 'cause my dad really likes that movie, even though it flops at the box office, you'll see. Oh, and we're going to have a black president in, like, thirty years."

"What in tarnation is this child saying?"

I hold up my hand to quiet him. "Wait, *and* the space shuttles will explode, and the Miami Heat will win the NBA championships."

"Miami gets a basketball team?" Officer Dale, who was quiet until now, looks super upset at this. I nod at him, and he puts his hand at his forehead in disgust.

"Phifer, would you shut it?" In-Charge practically cracks a whip at him to come back to his senses. "Miss, I don't know what on Earth you are talking about, but if this is some sort of smoke-and-mirrors attempt to distract us from the real matters at hand, you're going to—"

"Oh, and Disney is going to have two more theme parks soon—Hollywood Studios and Animal Kingdom—plus two new water parks, and . . ." Do I say it? They're already hanging off my every word. All I have is what I know. I need to use it. "River Country will be closed in 2001."

"What?" Gasps all around.

"Why are you saying all this? Who've you been talking to?" In-Charge's forehead looks like a road map from all the crisscrossing lines.

"Nobody."

There's a knock at the door, and they all stop to stare at who would be so bold as to interrupt such a damning foretelling event. Officer Chip-slash-Fred cracks the blinds open. He turns back to In-Charge. "It's the kid that was with her—the RC towel kid."

"Let him in."

Jason?

Fred unlocks the door, ushering him in. Jason stands boldly, like a defendant in front of a judge. My heart bursts with pride. "She's staying with me, Mr. Walsh."

"What are you doing?" I whisper at him, but he ignores me.

"What's your name again, son?"

"Jason Hewes, sir. She's a friend. She came to see me from Jupiter. My family and I are staying here during the summer. I work part-time at River Country." *Hewes?* I didn't know his last name. Now I feel even guiltier.

"You don't have to do this," I stage-whisper again, trying to get his attention, but his eyes are completely averted from mine.

"Well, Jason, if that's true—what loop are you staying in? I'm going to need your parents to come down and correct this situation, or else I'm forced to summon Orange County PD and press charges for her reckless behavior."

Officer Dale takes advantage of this little chat between In-Charge and Jason and squats down next to me, hanging on to the arm of the chair I'm in. "Does the National League win the World Series for the fourth time in a row this year? The Brewers take it?" He grins and nods hopefully.

"I don't know. I . . ."

"Phifer, I'm going to have to ask you to leave if you don't—"

"I'm sorry, sir. But it's obvious she has some sort of gift. I think we should listen. It may explain a few things."

"It explains nothing! Now go wait outside," In-Charge barks, and Officer Dale reluctantly obeys.

A gift, huh? Maybe people who claim to know the future and make money off it are really just time travelers who know because they've been there. They're making a living off knowing ordinary information.

Then In-Charge is yelling at all of them, and I take advantage of the momentary fight between them to look at Jason. He eyes me and whispers, "Bathroom . . . then *the* trailer."

Got it.

"Would you excuse me?" I say aloud, and everyone stops to stare at me. "I need to go use the ladies' room."

In-Charge's shoulder drops in annoyance. Could this meeting get any more off track for him? I shrug. "I'm sorry, but I really need to go!"

"Fred, accompany the young lady, please. And stand outside the door."

"Yes, sir," he says. I stand up, and Fred escorts me out into the hall, where Dale has been banished to time-out. He takes me to the end of the hall. "You're causing quite a ruckus. I've never seen him so upset. Just come clean, and everything will be fine."

"I am coming clean," I say, but Fred gives me a disapproving smirk. I step into the restroom and close the door. When I turn on the light, I'm immediately grateful for a fan that turns on, making a loud noise. I stop and take deep breaths. *What am I doing?*

Why did Jason want me to come in here?

I lean on the sink and stare into the mirror. I almost don't even recognize myself; that's how long it's been since I've even *cared* to look in a mirror. I have to get out of here. I can't wait for the police to come, but I can't leave Jason with the wolves in that office either. With my foot, I drop the toilet seat gently to mimic ordinary restroom sounds. After a minute I flush the toilet.

The trailer, he said. How does he expect me to get there with Fred waiting outside the bathroom door? Crap, was *bathroom* just a code word, and I was really supposed to make a run for it in the hallway? I mean, there's a small window, but I don't know if I can fit through it. And what if I get caught? How much worse can it get?

"Is everything okay in there?" Fred asks.

"Yes, I'm just feeling a little sick to my stomach. This is all so upsetting. Give me a minute."

"Okay."

I hop over to the window and pull on the latch, sliding the pane all the way to one side. I poke my head out to judge the height and survey the surroundings. There's a tram station and adjacent woods, but God only knows what's in there—snakes, possums, and raccoons, and not the fake kind. But what other choice do I have? Slowly, I hoist myself up to the window, which is hard to do when there's no sill, and there's nothing but aluminum siding between me and the outdoors.

With some necessary wiggling, I pull my body halfway through the window and slide gracelessly, headfirst, into the gravel below. I'm out. Quickly, I brush off my hands. All I need now is a flashlight beam on me, red and blue lights to flash, and I'm a certified criminal. But when I turn around, Jason's golf cart is right there waiting, key in the ignition and everything.

Yes, he meant for me to find this window.

If I take the cart, though, he won't have a way out if he needs it. He's already taken enough of the blame on my behalf as it is. From inside, I hear another knock at the bathroom door, louder this time. It's only a matter of time before Fred comes bursting in when he doesn't get a reply.

Up ahead, there's a tram pulling into the station. People start getting out. If I can blend in with them, I might be able to escape unseen. The only problem is most everyone is getting *off* it, carrying wet towels, beach bags, and sleeping children. I'd be one of only a handful getting on. Who would be heading into Fort Wilderness at this time?

But it's all I can do.

I have only seconds to do this. I take off running toward the tram, but I try not to look too desperate, lest I cause alarm with the driver. Just in time. I reach the tram and get on in the middle car, slumping low in my seat.

Please, please, God.

I can't live like this. I can't be a fugitive. I can't be distracting people and running all my life. I have to somehow force myself to leap again, even if it means leaping to another time altogether and starting all over again. But how can I leave Jason high and dry, taking the blame for everything? If I have another seizure, can I bring him back with me?

The tram driver mumbles, "All clear," and the train on wheels whisks off again. I need to stay low the whole way, but I also need to pay attention to the stops. We slow down, and the brakes screech softly. "Meadow Trading Post."

I need to get to Settlement Trading Post. *Ugh, come on, come on.*

A lot of people get on at this stop. A family with like four kids tries climbing into my row, but when they see me practically lying down, I shoo them, and they move to another row instead. A few cars drive around us slowly. I pull back from the window and pray that none of them contains Chip and Dale searching for me again.

We glide through the quiet main road, and minutes later we finally roll into . . . "Settlement Trading Post." I get off and run. Run, run, run down the street, stumbling, down another street, and through the loop I remember Jason driving when he was taking me to the abandoned trailer. It's even darker here without the lampposts, and I get a few curious looks from people hanging out in front of their trailers for a summer night's beer, but I keep running.

I think this is it.

I turn down another street where I remember seeing a trailer with the American flag in its window. Yes, this is it. I see the beige trailer up ahead and run up the steps, peeling back the doormat, looking for the key, the key, but it's not there. No! I check under the steps. Maybe it fell into the grass.

Suddenly the door above pops open, and I just about crap in my pants. I hide underneath the steps. Marsha—at least it looks like Marsha in the dark—runs out. She's crying. "Jerk, just leave me alone."

I feel like my lungs are going to explode inside my chest. *Calm down, Haley.* That strange sensation is back, the one where I feel like a light is starting to glow and cover me completely, and all I can do is try to breathe calmly, my back against the steps. No, I can't seize now.

I can't leave Jason back at the Mickey Police by himself like this.

"Baby, get back here." It's Jake standing above me, calling out.

"Go to hell, Jake. I ain't staying the night with you after all the chauvinist things you just said, and I ain't your baby!"

"I was kidding! I'm nice, baby, please. Just come here!" he yells.

Normally, I'd wait very still and not try to get caught, especially by Jake Hewes, Boy Scout–player wannabe. He'll only turn me in again. But I don't have a choice. I need to lie down. I need to stabilize myself. I need air.

"If you really are nice, then let me in," I say, out of breath.

"Who the hell is that?" he asks, and a moment later his mustached face appears as he crouches next to me. "Haley? What the hell?" He reaches over to help me stand. "You like to pop out of thin air, don't you?"

I accept his help to stand and lean against him. "You have no idea."

eighteen

Jake crouches next to me on the sofa. "All right, stay calm. Tell me what happened."

"I don't have time. I need you to make sure Jason is okay. He's at the police trailer down by check-in." I take deep breaths until I can see clearly again.

He bangs the back of the couch. "What? Not again. That boy can't stay out of trouble."

"No, it's my fault. He came to bail me out, only I escaped, and he's still there."

"You escaped security?" Jake shakes his head miserably. I suppose there's nothing worse in his eyes. He glances at the corded telephone on the TV stand.

"Don't. Please. Don't turn me in."

"I don't know else what to do with you, Haley. They're going to come around eventually, trailer by trailer, starting with all the unoccupied ones. You're going to have to go back to your family. Where are they again, Contemporary Resort?"

I see everybody knows my fake story by now. I have nothing to lose by telling him my real story. Everyone else knows it now anyway. "They're not here. I'm from another time, Jake. I slipped into the past by accident. I need to stay near River Country. That's why I was there the other night. I need you to help me, please."

Ugh, I sound crazy even to myself. He stares at me like I'm an alien from another planet, which might be easier to understand. Then he breaks into a forced laugh. "That is the dumbest thing I ever heard anybody say."

"Well, I'm glad the truth sounds dumb to you. I'll just be going, then." I get up to leave. He does nothing to stop me, only stands up too.

"So that thing"—he points to my phone, which is sitting on the kitchen counter right next to a beige shopping bag that says Radio Shack—"really is a phone from the future?"

My phone. I need that back. I need it on. I need Jason.

"Yes. Give me a place to hide, somewhere that's not a trailer, and once Jason gets it to turn on, I'll show you how it works."

He shakes his head. "I can't do that. I could lose my job for harboring a runaway."

"You mean, for helping someone?" I stare at him hard. It takes a special person to trust someone you've known only a few days, to

181

see that they're in need, not a hindrance. He's no Boy Scout, that's for friggin' sure. "I guess that's where your brother outshines you."

A look of shock crosses his face, then melts into hurt. Something tells me I'm not the first person to tell him that his so-called delinquent baby brother is a better person than he is, as much as he thinks he's doing the right thing. I do a quick check of my energy level. I'm still stressed out, but I don't feel the aura that precedes a seizure anymore. I can do this.

I get up calmly so as not to alarm him. "You know, your girlfriend is right." I shoot over to the counter, throw my phone inside the Radio Shack bag, and burst out the door. "You're not nice."

I run. And he runs after me. But I play baseball, and if there's anything I know how to do, it's pitch a mean curveball and run my ass off. I run, hearing his shouts behind me. "Haley, don't be stupid! You have nowhere to go! You need my help!"

"I haven't hurt you. Leave me alone!" In the murky darkness of the night, I nearly drop into a ditch full of leaves, but I swerve right in time.

"Fine, I'm not an asshole. I'll help you—*oof!*" And when I look over my shoulder, I see Jake, feet in the air, in the same ditch of leaves. "Ow!"

Oh my God, for real? I stop and turn around, hands on my knees, the Radio Shack bag dangling from my grip. "You will? How?"

"How, what?" Apparently, falling in the leaves has knocked his short-term memory right out of his skull.

"How can you help me?"

"I—" He holds his knee to his chest and twists his ankle around, as if testing it. "I can hide you near River Country."

"Where?"

"I'll show you." Awkwardly, he flips in the leaves, trying to gain leverage in the fluffy foliage. "Are you going to ask me if I'm okay?"

Cautiously, I walk toward him. This had better not be a trick. But from the way his face is squirming in pain, it's not. "Are you okay?"

"No."

I walk up to the shallow ditch and stare down at him. As much as they may not get along, Jason would not appreciate it if I didn't help his brother. I hold out my hand to help him up, praying that I don't get suckered into an act of betrayal. But I don't. Jake takes my hand and hoists himself out.

"Thanks."

"You're welcome."

"You didn't have to run, you know."

"You didn't have to be a jerk."

I have no idea where we're going. It feels like I'm headed to the Magic Kingdom on a little miniboat under the cover of darkness. How is this keeping me near River Country? But in a few minutes Jake pulls up to a dock on the north side of a small island between Fort Wilderness and the Contemporary Resort, an island I've seen in the future but never been to.

"Where are we?"

"Discovery Island."

"What *is* this place?"

"A nature preserve. There's birds, flowers . . . stuff to look at."

"Don't people work here? Won't they see me?"

"There's a place in the back where you can stay. If you're quiet and stay away from the pens and cages, nobody will ever know you're here."

"How do you know?"

He turns to me and scoffs. "You sure ask a lot of questions, don't you?"

"I want to know, to make sure you know what you're talking about." I take advantage of the darkness and smile a smart-ass smile, knowing he can't see me.

"It's where I used to hang out overnight sometimes before I discovered that old trailer. There, you happy?"

"I see. So, who's the happy trespasser now? You like breaking rules, is that what I'm hearing, Jake?"

He stands carefully and steps onto a wooden dock, taking a rope wrapped around a post and looping it through the metal grips on the miniboat. He reaches down and grips my arm, pulling me up to the dock with him.

"I guess you're not answering that."

"Follow me."

We walk down the gangplank and through two posts with tiki torches that are turned off. Already, birds start screeching and fluttering at our presence. Are those vultures? "I don't like this," I say.

"This is all I got. I'm friends with the folks who give the tours during the day. I can sneak back here and bring you food in the morning and tell my brother where you are. This might buy you one more night, but they'll find you eventually. You're going to have to turn yourself in." His words are like a punch to my stomach. "Or leave."

Of course he's right. What am I going to do? Hide near River Country indefinitely until I find my way back to the future? No. Eventually I'm going to have to give up and start living life in the eighties for the rest of my days. I'll miss my family, my friends, Jupiter, but, hey, at least I'll get to experience Michael Jackson and Mom's favorite movie, *Dirty Dancing*. That's something, right?

Following Jake through the winding sidewalks of Discovery Island, I realize I can't get away from here if they do find me. I don't have a boat, and it's impossible to swim away from the police, so this is pretty much it. My dead end. But for the same reasons, it's my salvation.

Jake must read my mind, because he whispers, "I doubt they'll come here looking for you. You'd be stupid to hide here." As if taking the ominous cue, a shipwrecked pirate ship appears out of the darkness on the beach of the island.

"That's the *Walrus*," Jake mumbles, gesturing to the ship.

"Doesn't look very walrus-y." I follow him into what appears to be the backstage area of the island. There's no pirate paraphernalia,

185

no crude-looking signs pointing this way or that, no roped bridges or fake pirate ships here.

Jake reaches a wooden door to a shed and opens it. Inside, there're some coils of rope, an old Discovery Island sign, and a life vest. He ushers me inside. "Your stateroom, mademoiselle."

"What? This is it?"

"This is it. What did you expect, a spa?"

"No, but . . ."

He walks in with me, maneuvers the life vest over to the blob of ropes, and points to it. "That'll make a great bed."

I turn to him, trying to make out his features in the dark. "Jake, I'm nervous. This place is creepy. I'm scared the employees will find me here in the morning."

"Trust me, just stay put. But if they do see you, tell them you're friends with Jake Hewes, the lifeguard from River Country," he says importantly. "They'll wonder what the hell's going on, but they won't turn you in." He rubs my arm, runs his hand down to my hand, and squeezes it.

"Thanks," I say, battling the urge to let it all out. *Stop, Haley. Time travelers do not cry.*

"Don't mention it. I'll have my brother come out here as soon as he can, so if you hear someone walking around, look through this hole first." He points to a crack in the wooden door, a crack he's probably peeped through many a time, it seems. "And make sure it's him."

"And if it's not?"

He laughs softly. "What's the worst that could happen? They're not going to shoot you, Haley. This is Disney." He turns around and leaves, and for the rest of the night, I'm left with the sounds of birds, crickets chirping, soft waves against the shore, and the realization that he didn't take back my phone.

nineteen

I know it's sunrise when birds start squawking at each other. My nerves, having calmed the last few hours, flare up again. The avian residents of the island are excited for the start of a new day, but I am hiding in a shed, awaiting my fate. Yes, fate. Because for once, it all seems entirely out of my hands.

For all I know, cast members may already be here on the island, feeding the animals and preparing for a full day of touring. One of them may suddenly decide he needs extra rope and remember that there's some out in this wooden shed. Then, surprise!

My stomach grumbles like crazy. What happens if neither Jake nor Jason shows up? How do I get out of here by myself? A minute later I hear shuffling outside. I hop to my feet and cautiously peer out the hole in the door. I don't see anyone. Maybe it's a seagull looking for its own breakfast. If it's a vulture, it can just wait for me to die of fear in here, then feed off my carcass.

Then there's a scratching sound on the door, and I freeze.

I can feel someone standing outside the door. It's not a seagull. "Haley," someone whispers.

The door creaks open, and there's Jason, wearing the same Police shirt he was wearing the night before, with a brown paper bag in his hands. He has dark circles under his eyes, dark circles I know I caused.

"Jason!" I pull him inside and throw my arms around him. My fingers hook into his hair, and I just want him to take me somewhere, anywhere, I don't care, as long as we're together. I couldn't care less about whatever food he's brought me. He pulls back and kisses me. I melt into his kiss, and for a few moments nothing else matters.

Nothing.

"You have to go, Haley." His breath is soft and sweet against my face.

"I told you I don't have anywhere to go."

"I mean, out of Disney. You have to leave." He tugs at my hair, framing my face with it.

"I can't. I have to stay near River Country. I think it's my portal for going home. What happened after I left that office?"

He sighs heavily and collapses to the ground. "They asked me to bring my parents, but I had to confess that my dad is nonresponsive. It's just me and Jake. Been for a while."

"What?" I pull away and look him in the eye. "What does that mean, nonresponsive?"

He shrugs, then looks to the floor. "My mom died, Haley. Two years ago—overdose. My dad just sits in his chair, doesn't speak to anyone. Me, I've had a rough couple of years. That's why Jake is obsessed with keeping me—us—on the straight and narrow."

"Straight and narrow," I repeat. "What does that mean? I can't think."

"Keeping me in line. So I don't want them to find you here. I don't know if you're telling me the truth or not, about coming from the future. I don't know *what* the hell's happening anymore, but I know I want you safe."

I hold on to his shoulders and press my face against his chest, finding comfort in the rhythmic beating of his heart. Outside, the new sound of rain sloshes on the roof of the shed, and just as quickly, humidity seeps in through the opening of the door. "What if I stay?" I propose. "What if I live with you? I mean, if your dad won't mind." It's a possibility. I might be crazy for even considering it, but if I can't leap back to 2014, then Jason's all I've got.

"You can't."

"Why not?"

He pulls back and holds me at arm's distance. "Because I have to leave too."

"*What?* Why?"

"They fired me, Haley."

I stare at him. He isn't kidding. "But you didn't do anything wrong!"

"Actually, I did. I helped you hide instead of bringing you *to their attention sooner*," he says, mocking someone's tone, probably In-Charge's. "Not wrong to me, but obviously to them."

I can't believe this. I got Jason fired from his job, the job that was supposed to save him and get him back on the right path. I ruined everything. In allowing myself to have a summer fling while I was stuck here, I ruined his life. My dad is right. I'm totally selfish.

"I'm leaving tomorrow morning," Jason says. "They'll be at my trailer tonight to make sure I've packed up all my stuff."

"But where will you go?" My heart feels like it's going to split into pieces, and he can keep them all. They're all his anyway.

"Army, I guess."

"No, Jason." I shake my head. Nothing wrong with the army, except . . . that isn't his dream. "Study first. Write about your mom dying on the college applications. Tell them how you want to be something. Come on, Jason. You can't just give up on your dreams."

He turns away from me and rests in the open doorway, arm up on the frame. "It's not that easy."

"Okay, what about ROTC then? Don't they, like, pay for your college, then you work for them, but after your obligation is done, you're free, right? Isn't that how it works?"

"I think so. I don't know. I'll see."

"Why can't I come with you?" I plead.

I want to. I want to stay with Jason and support him, after

everything he's done for me, stuck out his neck for me, got *fired* for me, and on the Fourth of July, no less. It's the least I can do.

I want to let the big tears out. I want them to push up past my throat and spill before I can do anything to stop them. Why can't I? Not since my parents split up six years ago have I been able to really cry. I've been so numb. But I could do this. I could make being in 1982 work, be with Jason, somehow. I come up behind him and wrap my arms around his torso. "I don't want to lose you."

"I don't want to lose you either, Haley, but you have parents who care about you. You don't know how special that is. After I'm gone, you must find your way home. But if you're still stuck here after I leave, stay with my brother and wait for me, okay?"

Ugh. I can't say I don't care about my parents, because I do. I care a lot. But they've lived; they would understand if I found love and didn't want to ever let it go. They wouldn't be able to blame me. But waiting around with Jake for Jason to finish with the army doesn't sound like how I want to spend my life. "God, this sucks."

He laughs and turns around to hug me. "Listen, we'll have one last day together." He's not done, but already his words are making me cringe. "And we'll have a blast. We'll do whatever you want. We'll watch the fireworks tonight. We'll watch them from the beach, or stay here, if you prefer." He kisses me long and sweet. I know just what he means. And I can't say I disagree with his plan. Watching the fireworks with Jason in this hidden spot where anything can happen is very much in line with how I feel right now.

I think about Marsha's words the first day I arrived, how Jason had not wanted to hook up with anyone so far this summer, and how that made me the pick of the litter. I'm happy knowing that he decided to spend his time with me, that whatever he felt was too fragile and special to share with just anyone, he chose to share with me.

And if this has all been a dream after all, so be it. It's how I'd want the dream to end.

"But, Jason, before you leave, I need you to do something for me."

"Something else?" He smiles and kisses me again. I feel the pull of his body, drawing me in, making me dizzy.

I pull away and touch his mouth with a fingertip. "I need you to turn on my phone."

He taps his forehead. "Oh, that's right. Where did my brother put all that stuff? Damn, now I have to go get it."

I run over to my makeshift bed and pick up the plastic Radio Shack bag I brought with me. "It's all right here."

"Radical." He comes over and looks inside. "Five-volt, wires, okay, but I need a soldering gun. Idiot doesn't think I can connect wires without soldering them, does he? Can I see your telephone?" I hand him the phone, and he inspects it, staring into the charging slot for a long while, mumbling to himself. "This looks nothing like a phone. Wait here, Haley. I'm going to go search for a soldering gun, and I'll be back soon. Eat what I brought you. Oh, and here, take this. . . ."

He pulls a folded map of Discovery Island from his pocket. I must say I'm excited to have something to look at in my dungeon besides a life vest. "Yay, a treasure map," I say.

He unfolds it and points to a spot near the *Walrus* pirate ship. "You're on Shipwreck Beach. If you have to run, wait outside this trail until you see a group of tourists. The guide will start talking about the wildlife that lives in these parts. You can slide in through the trees here, and nobody will ever notice that you weren't part of the group already."

"Okay, but it's still raining. I'll probably stay here."

"Good idea." He kisses me one last time, and then he's gone again, leaving me with my empty shed, my dead phone, and some light reading.

I'm not one to sit around, even if it is waiting for Jason to come back, so as soon as I've read the entire map three or four times and it stops raining, I venture out of the shed as quietly as possible. I feel exposed, as if everyone on every boat crossing Bay Lake and every guest at River Country, a mere hundred yards away, can see me.

It's not a big island, but they've packed a lot to see into such a small space. I can't believe I've gone by this place on a boat to the Magic Kingdom at least three times before in my life and never even knew it was here. I thought it was an unoccupied, uninhabited place. It's like a secret jewel. I love it already.

I cross over the South Creek Inlet and spot the first people of the day, a girl and a guy wearing gloves and carrying buckets. They're busy opening cages and distributing feed. For a moment I think the girl sees me, but she's only perking up to hear an announcement made on a radio. I stay away, heading a little farther down the beach.

There's the sound of water rushing. Following it means squeezing between trees, which I do, and I am immediately rewarded with the prettiest sight of the day.

A tall mass of rocks, real rocks, not the engineered, stage kind over at River Country, looms over me, and right between two of the biggest formations rushes a little waterfall, a lovely treasure in the middle of Discovery Island. I want to whip out my phone and take a picture, it's so pretty, but I curse at the impossibility. I hope Jason will change that soon. I sit here for the longest time, hearing the sounds of people in the distance, guides talking about parrots and flamingos and lemurs. There're lemurs here? As with River Country, I wonder why this attraction isn't open in my time either.

A melancholy sadness comes over me. If it weren't for my family, I think I'd stay here, as absurd as the thought may be. But I wouldn't be able to live on Discovery Island anyway. I may as well enjoy this moment, because quiet interludes in natural settings are few and far between. Tonight, everything will change. Whether or not I can re-create the conditions necessary for jumping back to my time, it'll be Jason's last night here. And right now, for me, Jason *is* Fort Wilderness.

As much as I'd love to hang out in this private spot all day, I need to get back in case Jason returns with the soldering gun. Where does he plan on plugging that in, anyway? I'm heading back to Shipwreck Beach when I hear chatter about which animals to feed and when right around the corner. I duck back into the trees to keep from being seen. After the voices become muffled, I emerge and run down the beach to my shed. But there's something there now that wasn't there before.

A light blue speedboat, like the one I came on last night with Jake, is perched on the sand. Someone bursts out of the shed frantically, and though my heart jumps into my throat, it's only Jason. "Holy crap, Haley, you scared me. I thought you got caught." He comes up to me and pulls me by the arm. "Come on, get in. We can't charge this thing out here."

He hands me the Radio Shack bag, and I hop into the speedboat. As soon as we pull away, someone spots and points to us. "Right there, see them?" I overhear a girl wearing a tropical flowered shirt say.

A cast member dude emerges from the trees, shielding his eyes from the sun.

"Crap, they see us. What do we do?" I ask.

"We wave," Jason says. And he does with a smile and points to his River Country name tag pinned to his shirt. I wave too. We casually smile and wave, smile and wave. The couple of cast members see that it's all fine, that the two unauthorized people who just left the island are one (fake) cast member and one (fired) cast member. They smile and wave back. It's all good.

"Wow. Amazing how well that trick works."

"No kidding."

"So where are we going to do this? People are bound to notice."

"I haven't the foggiest idea," Jason says, pulling into the marina not one minute later.

I want to laugh. He sounds a bit like my dad with some of his sayings. I suppose the way I talk will sound funny to someone thirty years from now too, so I shouldn't judge. He helps me up onto the docks, and together we walk, for the first time, I think, holding hands out in public. Jason is unusually quiet, contemplative, and I wonder what he's thinking.

Down the boardwalk, over to the Settlement Trading Post, and down behind the general store we go. He stops and looks around, his eyes scanning the grounds.

"Okay, now what?" I ask.

His eyes stop at an electrical post for charging golf carts. "There. I hope this one has power." He looks around, presumably to make sure nobody is coming, and crouches in front of the post.

I crouch too and open the bag for him. "What do you need first?" I ask, excited for this experiment to begin.

"The five-volt power source. That one." He points to a black charger that looks like something that might charge a video camera. He takes it and bites down on the adapter at the end.

"You're going to eat it?" I tease.

He glances up at me with those blue eyes, and I relish the thought that he wants to admonish me for my smart mouth. He rips off the adapter and surrounding plastic, exposing two live wires. "Plug this in, please." He pulls out of his pocket a soldering gun and hands it to me.

"Whoa, where'd you get this?" I plug the gun into the electrical post.

"Boat rentals. I asked if they had one, and they said no. So I asked to use their restroom and found one in the back."

I cock my head at him. "You are just MacGyver, aren't you?"

"Who?" I thought I was being clever by quoting something eighties, but I guess that show hasn't started yet from the quizzical look he's giving me.

"Nothing. Okay, so it's plugged in. Now what?"

"Now, reach in my other pocket and find a small coil of wire." He angles his body toward me so I can fish around in his shorts.

"Um, why am I doing this when you have a free hand?" I ask, biting my lip.

He laughs, and I pull out the thick metal wire wound tightly. "You're the one who fell for it. Okay, now hold your phone out. Before I melt this, let me make sure these are the pins that need to connect. Stay away from the live ends." He plugs in the power converter and slowly comes toward the phone in my hand, inserting the two exposed wires into the slot where the charger would connect.

Nothing happens.

He takes them out and moves them over to another spot. "I think it's this one. I hope five volts isn't too much and I don't fry the board."

"Why? What happens if you fry the board?"

He looks at me and raises an eyebrow. "You stay here with me forever."

I take in his sexy look. "Fry the board, then." My words make him smile, and the way the corners of his mouth pull out and up makes my stomach flip. He holds the wires very still for a minute.

"I don't think it's working." Jason scoffs, but right when it seems he's going to pull it off and try another spot, I see the dead battery symbol appear on my screen, indicating that the phone will soon turn on if left to charge.

"That's it! That's the one!" I clap and cover my mouth, noticing some people walking nearby.

"Whoa. That is so cool." The way Jason's eyes light up momentarily makes my heart dance around. And that's just at seeing the battery symbol! Wait till he sees the rest! "So here, hold this." He unplugs the five-volt power source and hands me the stripped wire ends. "You're going to hold these wires right there, right where they made it turn on, and I'm going to solder them in place. Ready?"

"Ready."

"Don't move a muscle. If I burn it, we're screwed."

I hold the two together, and I must admit, I'm having fun hot-wiring my iPhone. He takes the soldering gun, holds it to the coiled wire, and melts the very end of it. Then, gently, he brings the liquid metal drop to the spot where the exposed wires meet the last two pins and fuses them together. "Blow," he says.

"Is this another trick?" I ask.

"Just blow." He smiles, and I blow cool air onto the drop until it hardens.

"Okay, I think that should work." He unplugs the soldering gun and replugs the power source. He claps once and rubs his hands together. "Let's see this telephone of yours, Haley-Haley." The quiet dead battery symbol is back.

"Cell phone, Jason-Jason."

"Whatever. It's the future, and I'm about to see it because of you."

I smile and put my arm around him. We sit down cross-legged and wait while the phone charges. "Does that mean you believe me now?"

"I don't know. The jury is still out. I still think you might be an imaginative lunatic. And to think I really believed your story about your dad being an inventor. I was actually a little jealous."

"Why? You want to invent something?" I bump him with my shoulder.

"Well, the thought of being the first to do something has always appealed to me, sure."

Hmm, if he sticks with me all day . . . "You might just get your wish," I say quietly. I want to show him the waterfall I found, and after that we'll have the shed on the beach all to ourselves.

"Oh yeah?" His eyes widen with interest.

"Yeah." I lean my head on his shoulder, watching the battery symbol filling up with red. "You see that? That means it's charging."

"That's amazing."

"You ain't seen nothing yet. Wait till it turns on."

He pulls my chin up to look right at me. "I wasn't talking about the phone. I was talking about you. Letting me be your first."

"Oh."

He kisses me again, holding my head and bringing my face closer to him, when suddenly I hear the familiar chime of an iPhone coming back to life, the most beautiful sound I've heard in a while. I can take pictures, I can take video, I can show him apps, though I can't use half of them, since there're no cellular networks. But still, it's the only thing here that's from my time besides me!

"What was that?" He tears away and looks down at the black screen with the glowing white apple in the middle of it.

I take the phone and place it in his hands. This might be the end. A boy with an electronic gadget in his hand, one with technology from thirty years in the future. We'll probably never have a conversation or look into each other's eyes again. "That, my friend . . ." I say, "is the sound of something way, *way* more *rad* than your precious Commodore 64."

twenty

We sit there for about an hour while he plays Angry Birds, Jelly Car, and basically opens and closes every app on my phone. I have to show him how to swipe, and he looks funny doing it, pressing down hard like the screen is a button or something. I have to keep looking over our shoulders to make sure nobody is watching.

"This is the coolest shit I've ever seen," he mumbles, his eyes never ripping away from the screen. "This looks so realistic. Look at the feathers on this bird!"

"And this is only half of it," I tell him. "The other half needs a network to work right, but it doesn't exist yet. With it, you can send messages, call people, see the weather in any city. . . . It's really cool, Jason. It's communication at your fingertips. You would really love my time." Jason would be about fifty in my time. He would've already mastered all these things, but for now, it's awesome watching him discover it all.

"What's this one here?" He points to an app called WDW Waits with a castle on it.

"That tells you how long the waits are in the Disney parks. See, you can click on Magic Kingdom, EPCOT, Animal Kingdom, Hollywood Studios, and it tells you the wait times for each ride."

"Are those new parks?"

"Yeah," I say, even though they're not really *new* anymore. "There's four, and two water parks."

"What about River Country?" he asks. I don't know what to tell him, and after a few moments of my silence, his blue eyes fall on me, waiting.

"River Country closed, Jason. Around 2001," I say, pressing my lips together. "It's still there, but it's all covered in vines, trees . . . like nature reclaimed the land. It's really odd, because from what I've seen, it was a lot of fun."

The hurt is evident in his eyes and the way he seems to wince at the news. "Why'd they close it?"

I shrug. "Not sure. In fact, I don't know anybody our age who knows about River Country. I only knew a little about it because my dad mentioned it sometimes." *My dad, that guy Oscar, who hangs out with your brother and Marsha,* I almost tell him, but I can't. For some reason, this privy information feels too sacred to share. "A lot happens in thirty years."

He looks off toward the beach and shakes his head. "Don't tell me. I'm not sure I want to know more."

"I wouldn't want to know either." Which is probably why we would never be able to stay together. I would know too much.

We're quiet for a while as I lean into him and watch him play with my phone. Every so often, he lifts it, peeks into the charger slot and the headphone jack. "You should buy stock in Apple," I tell him with a wink. "Once you have enough money."

"No kidding." He looks at his watch, gets on his feet, and holds out his hands to help me up. "Come on, Haley. We don't have much time left." He crouches to where the phone is plugged in and unplugs the power converter. "I guess it's off for now."

"No, it'll stay on. It's charged for at least a good five, six hours."

He shakes his head in amazement. "It holds the charge for that long? I wonder why it doesn't just use double A batteries."

"It wouldn't have the sleek design if it did."

"Ah," he says, and I break off the soldered wires from the charging pins.

"Where should we go?" I ask, sliding the phone back into my pocket. My hands get a little sweaty at the thought of what he may suggest, but I'm ready. Anywhere alone with Jason would be totally fine.

"Wherever you want," he says, taking me by the hand and wandering over to the marina. I hold on to his hand tightly and lean against his arm. I'm not ready for him to leave me just yet.

"Should we be out in the open like this? They're probably looking for me."

"Then let's hide," he says.

"Take me back to Discovery Island. I want to show you something," I say.

"Oh yeah? What is it?"

"Come." I lead him over to the little blue boats we escaped on earlier. Jason shows an employee his cast member ID, and the guy just lets him into the speedboat. He drives us past River Country, where a lagoon full of people are having a hell of a time sliding, swimming, and sunbathing. I take a long, hard look at it, in case I never see it this way ever again.

Sigh . . . River Country.

We disembark at Shipwreck Beach and run to the trees before anyone can see us. The sun is starting its midafternoon descent in the west, and my heart aches knowing I don't have much more time with Jason before he needs to leave.

"So what is it you want to show me?" he asks.

I walk him to the path where I found myself earlier and watch his eyes widen with amazement at the little waterfall hidden behind the trees and rocks. "Isn't it cool?" I ask. "I stumbled upon this all by myself. Tell me you didn't know about it, or you'll break my heart."

"I swear, I didn't know about Minnie Falls," he says, smiling.

I jab his arm with a finger. "Aww, that's not nice. Just pretend I'm showing you something in Disney that you didn't already know about."

We walk up to the falls, and I hold out my hand, letting the cool water run over it. I rub the dampness over my face and neck, loving the feeling on my sweaty skin. He takes my hand and presses it against his face. "Let's just rename it Haley Falls, for the girl who thinks she discovered it." He smiles, and I jab him again.

"Stop!" But he grabs my hand and playfully twists my arm behind my back. I shriek, and he covers my mouth with a strong hand. In one fell swoop, he reaches under me and lifts me in his arms. Next thing I know, I'm headed straight for the rushing water. "No! Jason, stop!" I laugh and scream at the same time.

"Shh, they're going to hear you. Say 'uncle.'"

"Uncle! Aunt, whatever!" I whisper, but it does no good. He's holding me inches away from the water, and I'm getting wet regardless.

"I don't know," he says. "That didn't sound sincere to me." He leans me out farther into the water, and I'm hitting and punching his chest and shoulder.

"Stop! Stop, Jason," I laugh. "*My phone!* Stop!" He realizes the importance of this and grants me a few seconds to pull it out of my pocket and slide it into a grassy knoll next to the waterfall. Then it's no use to protest. He drops me right into the water, but I make sure, before I hit the cold creek, to grab on to his shirt and pull him down too. Boom! Right there with me.

Bubbles all around, billowy silence that reminds me of when I fell into the River Country lagoon, only Jason is with me now, all wet shorts and shirt. I come up for air right when he does. "Oh, you're gonna get it now, Haley-Haley."

"Am I?" I tease.

He smiles a crooked half smile, nodding and peeling off his shirt, throwing it onto the grass. My shirt is suddenly heavy on me, a barrier between me and his skin, but I don't feel right peeling it off, considering we could get caught at any moment by cast members, Mickey Police, or worse—real police—so I roll the sleeves up around my shoulders, and the bottom, I twist and tuck up underneath my bra.

Then his arms are around my waist, pulling me in, and my hands have no choice but to rest against his tanned arms and chest.

So intoxicating. So lovely.

We kiss.

This moment. *This* is what matters.

His hand is in my hair, twisting and kneading it into a rope, as he kisses me. He breaks the kiss but rests his forehead against mine. "Whatever happens," he says, wiping water from my face, "I love you."

And even though I've never told those words to any guy before, this time I don't even think about them. They just roll out. Because I do. A hundred percent. Agree. "I love you too," I say, watching his water-beaded lips turn into a shadowy smile as the sun shining behind him casts a forever kind of glow on him. "Whatever happens."

We kiss again, and this time I feel his body press against mine, and if it weren't for the possibility of being caught here, I would so peel the rest of his clothes right off him. "Want to go somewhere else?" I ask.

He nods, pulling me even closer toward him, putting his

arms around me and holding me in a long hug. What's coming is inevitable, and I'm dizzy just thinking about it. Part of me wants to start asking questions—has he done this before, with whom, and how many? And part of me thinks like him, not wanting to know the future, that I don't care what's in the past. It doesn't matter. Because call me crazy, but I think that no matter who he's been with, no one's mattered more than me, and I'd have to say the same.

Suddenly there's a noise around the rocks, the sound of pails and gates locking, and Jason shushes me, finger to his lips. "We can't stay here," he whispers. My heart hurts. A lot. Regardless of where we go or what we do, we can never be alone for long. And something I've been trying to ignore makes its way front and center to the rational part of my brain—as perfect as this moment feels, we are always . . . hiding. None of this is meant to be.

"But where can we go?" I ask.

"Let's separate for now. You go back to the shed and wait for me there."

"Why?" I ask, hearing the panic in my voice. "Where are *you* going to be?"

"I'm going to run and check to make sure nobody is looking for you. Then I'm going to stop at the trailer, check on my dad, and pack a few things. I'll be back with food, and we'll hang out before . . ."

Before he leaves.

He sees the look of dread on my face, and he holds my chin and kisses me softly. "Don't be sad, Haley. If it's meant to be, we'll see each other again. But I need to get out of here for now. They said they wouldn't hold anything against me if I left quietly. I can't have another blemish on me; you understand, don't you?"

I nod, clinging to his hands. "What time will you come back?"

"Before the fireworks. We'll watch them together."

Something about the way he says it kills me deep inside. What if he doesn't come back? Should I really be allowing myself to feel all these complicated feelings if he's just going to run off and never come back? Why invest in people when nothing lasts forever?

If he doesn't come back, it's okay, Haley.

You loved him.

While he was here.

"I promise," he says, his eyes capturing the sunlight off the water and breaking it into a million colors, and I swear I can see every single one of them right now.

"Okay," I say, nodding. He smiles sadly and turns, hoisting himself out of the water.

"I'll go first. Wait, like, five minutes, then check if the coast is clear. If you don't see anyone, run back to the shed. Be back soon." I watch him retrieve his shirt, drape it around his shoulders, crane his neck out between the rocks, then disappear, taking the beauty of Haley Falls with him.

I stay there for a bit, alone with the sound of crashing water, watching the spot where he stood a moment ago, imagining him still there, and it dawns on me how cold I feel once he's gone. Something else dawns on me—I want to go home after tonight. Because if Jason won't be here anymore, then I don't want to be here either.

After a few minutes I climb out of the water, wringing my shirt out as well as the thick rope of my hair. At the rocks' opening, I check to make sure no one is around, then head out. I make it back to my shed and throw myself onto my makeshift bed. So exhausted.

I wonder how long I would be able to live on this island like a real shipwrecked girl with real shipwrecked shorts and never be found. I fall into sleep, not full sleep, but am always aware of the water's lapping on the shore and the caw of the birds on the island. Not sure how much time goes by, but it must be a couple of hours, judging from the changing hues of sunlight outside—yellow, tangerine, blood orange. . . .

When is Jason coming back?

I slide my body to be able to see through the crack in the door. For when the blue boat reappears. For when I see his legs, his body, making his way back to me. Maybe about four hours go by altogether. The sun is now low, creating long stretchy shadows in the sand made by the shed.

If Jason's not here, I want to go home.

I sit up.

Is that it? Is that the trigger? When I stood outside the gated wall of River Country, I *wanted* to be inside more than anything. So much, I could hear it, see it. If Jason leaves, I'll *want* to go home.

Suddenly some long shadows interrupt my thoughts, becoming more human shaped.

And then the shadows start pointing their fingers, talking in men's voices. "You go that way. We'll check the west end."

I freeze.

They're looking for me.

The sound of my own heartbeat magnifies in my ears. My stomach clenches, and the little shed feels tinier than the amount of air I need to breathe. As much as I should stay in and hide, I feel the walls closing in. An aura of light creeps around the edges of my peripheral vision, and I know that if I don't bust out of here and get fresh air now, I'll slip into the familiar unconsciousness caused by stress.

And possibly leave this place and time.

Just like I wanted to three days ago.

Before I fell.

For Jason.

twenty-one

I'm almost relieved by the opposite directions they take, until I hear someone talking into a walkie-talkie right outside my hideout. "The guests have all left. We're going to comb out here now, over."

"Copy that. Let us know what you find."

Ugh. If I wait for them to open the door and find me, that'll be the end. But if I escape now, I can bank on the hope that my athletic skills will let me outrun them.

It doesn't really sound like much of a choice.

I'm out.

Carefully, I push the front door as softly as I can, taking a quick inventory of my surroundings then squeezing through the space. I realize suddenly that I left my flip-flops inside the shed, but I can't turn around now. Every second is of the essence.

I see them walking down the beach, their backs turned. Two of them are headed toward the *Walrus*, and three of them, in the direction of Haley Falls. I can just barely see the top of the lookout's head, the one standing next to the shed. He's turned and watching the shoreline instead of checking out the *inside* of the shed. Luck has thrown me a bone.

I pad off in the sand. Where to go, I have no idea. I walk in the direction of the island's general public exit. Lampposts are turning on. The sky is purple to the north and dark blue to the east. Only a ribbon of orange remains in the west. Fantasy in the Sky is going to start soon, but Jason has not returned.

Why isn't he here yet? That couldn't have been the last time I saw him. I never even got to take a picture with him! This isn't fair! *Pictures . . . I left my phone in the shed! Damn it, I can't go back for it.*

There's a rope bridge to my left. I head toward it since it's hidden between two walls of trees. But it's not long before I see someone—a lady up ahead wearing a safari hat and looking cast-memberish. When she turns to gaze at me curiously, I see her oval name tag with the Mickey head resembling a globe with grid line. Yup. Park employee.

"Miss? Can I help you?" she asks, smiling politely but clearly puzzled as to why I'm still here when all the guests have left.

"Where do I get the boat off the island? Sorry, I lost my folks and got totally disoriented." I smile sheepishly, proud of my use of the word *folks*.

She thinks about this for a minute, and it seems like she's about to point me in the direction of the pier, when she cocks her head. Naturally, her eyes fall on my frayed Daisy Dukes. "Are you the one they're looking for?"

"What? No, of course not," I lie. "Never mind, I remember where the pier is now. I just hope my family isn't too worried about me." I wave and shuffle past her, but this is a performance that can go only so far. In a few moments she's telling someone else about me as I'm running down the path, and when I look back, there're three of them, and one of them—an older man—is holding a walkie-talkie to his mouth.

"Damn it," I mutter, running past a wading pool with flamingos, a tree with lots of screeching birds, and a few cages with I don't know what else, because I'm moving too fast to care.

"Hold it right there," a blond man says to my left, startling me. But I pick up speed and jump off the path, into trees, through knee-deep canals, past crates painted to look old. He's behind me. I can hear him telling the others to catch up with us in the direction I'm headed.

Thanks for the tip, buddy.

So I break right to avoid them and sprint through the trees like there're two outs in the tenth inning and my run will win the game. I burst out the opposite end of this clump of trees. I don't know where I'm headed. Just trying to lose them. My only hope is to find Haley Falls and hide there until they leave. But I don't know where that is anymore, and it's hard to pass up the empty light blue, red, and yellow speedboats banked on the beach.

I make a break for them, sloshing into the water and pulling the blue one back with me. *Is there a key? I need a key.* . . . Yes, it's in the ignition in the off position. I turn it on, hearing the boat groan to life. But then the men emerge on the beach running my way. This won't work if they jump into the other two boats. Quickly, I hop out again and, using all the strength I have left in my legs, push the other boats into the water with my foot. Once they're afloat, I give them another push until they drift out in the bay. Anyone can still climb into them, but now they'll have to wade out into the water first.

"Miss, Walt Disney World authorities. Stop where you are!" they call out to me.

"Yeah, I know, I know," I mutter, sitting at the wheel and pushing the throttle forward. The back end of the boat sinks slightly into the water as it picks up speed, and I must say, I am quite impressed with my 007 getaway and my total runaway attitude!

"Miss, I said stop where you are!"

This is awful. I'm running from the law. My dad would be so ashamed; my mother, so proud. Here I go. . . . I turn and speed straight for the marina, until I notice that the employee there has been informed of my whereabouts from the way he's waving his arms for me to stop. So I turn the speedboat right onto the sandy beach across from Pioneer Hall instead. There're a million people here sitting on the sand, in beach chairs, lying in hammocks, all waiting for the Fourth of July fireworks to begin. The perfect place to blend in.

Some people scatter, and I get a few odd looks, but I step out and run through the sand, weaving between the groups of people. For a moment I stop behind a big cypress tree to catch my breath. The aura is fighting its way to my vision again. I wish I had my meds. *No, do not give in to it, Haley. Not now. Not before you see Jason one more time.*

When I peek around the tree, the officials from Discovery Island are already docking and jumping off, looking for me. A few people point in my direction, and the men set out after me. Crap, crap! That's it. It's time to run full throttle. I book it.

All the way past the Settlement Trading Post, taking the short-cut to Jason's trailer I remember from yesterday morning. Seems so long ago. They're behind me. I can hear their frantic voices on their walkie-talkies. Why am I running, anyway? My breath is loud in my ears. The orange glow ebbs and flows in my peripheral vision.

I feel like I've done this before. Like I've been chased before. I hear people talking who are not there, concerned voices in my ear from somewhere beyond. *Haley? Haley, can you hear me?* "No," I mumble. "No, no, no."

So tired. I just want to sit down and rest. But I can't. I can't. Have to keep moving. Through a loop where the smells of BBQ hit me like a pile of bricks. I run past rows and rows of beige trailers. I think it was this way, but I don't know where I am anymore. All I want to do is lie down. So exhausted. So overwhelmed.

I stop for one second, just one second . . . hands on my knees, breathing deep . . . in and out . . . in and out . . . in through the nose, out through the mouth. Gotta keep moving. I stand back up and turn around and smack into someone. I scream out loud and struggle, wrestling my arms out of their hold.

"So sorry. Are you okay?" That voice. Love that voice. He lets go of my arms. "Haley?"

I look up and see that face. That beautiful, surfer boy voice. "Jason?" I throw my arms around him. "They're chasing me. I can't do this anymore. I can't." This is too much. I've never been under so much pressure in my life. This is worse than the FCAT, yet this hasn't made me seize in three days. Talk about resistance building.

"Haley, baby . . ."

"Take me with you, Jason," I beg, biting my lip to keep from losing it. "I'll go with you wherever you go. I can't be here anymore. Please, just let me come with you."

"You can't come with me, Haley. Where would you go?"

"The army, wherever. I don't care."

He smiles sadly at the ridiculousness of what I'm saying. "Just face them, Haley. What's the worst that could happen? They take you down to the station, they try to find your parents . . . eventually services will come get you, but it's better than running from them."

"No!" I cry. "I can't. I can't live this way. If I can't be with you, then I have to find a way back home. This place isn't for me. I've only stuck it out as long as I have because of you."

The group of men break through the trees right as the first firework booms into the sky behind them. From far away I hear cheers from the beach crowd. The men slow down once they see they've found me, and I'm not running anymore. "Okay, that's enough, miss. Come with us. We're not here to hurt you."

"She just needs a minute," Jason says to them, holding his hand up.

"No!" I say again, tears welling up in my eyes. I fling them away. "I'm going with you," I demand.

The blond man comes up to me, and from behind me, I hear, "Thank you, Taylor. We'll take it from here." It's In-Charge from the Mickey Police. He's strolling up to me, smile on his face. "And you," he says, pointing at Jason, "I believe you're supposed to have vacated by now."

"I was just leaving, sir. It's okay to say good-bye, isn't it?" Jason's so polite and snarky at the same time. I love him for it. He turns to me and holds my hands. "Haley . . ." I swear, I'm going to faint. This doesn't feel real anymore. It's a dream. It has to be. A dream I've had before.

More fireworks boom into the sky. More cheers erupt. On the loop road, guests are running for the paths, hurrying to see the show that's already started. Smells of roasted corn, hot dogs, charred burgers . . .

"Haley, go with them. It'll be okay, I promise. You haven't done anything wrong."

"How can you let me go?" I ask. I can't help but feel like he's abandoning me. But he's right. Of course he is. I know it. I've hit a brick wall, a dead end; there's no way out of this. His face, his gorgeous face, swerves in front of me. One second it's here, and the next it's two inches to the right.

If I can't be with you, I don't want to be here. I want to go home.

And because I need more stress, a police car pulls into the street and turns on its red and blue lights. No siren. Wouldn't want to alarm the guests. Only the lights are left on—flashing—red and blue, red and blue, red and blue. . . .

Flashing in my face. My eyes.

Red and blue.

How can you let me go? my voice echoes. *No control . . . let go. . . .*

Jason's voice from somewhere far away. "Because I love you, Haley."

Fireworks boom, sparkles of light, fizzling, dissipating. Cheers.

Jason's arms around me. *I love you.*

I fall.

Haley . . .

His hand cradling my head.

Bright white. Flickers of light.

Silence.

twenty-two

She's moving."

Who is?

"Haley." Someone I know. Someone familiar to me is talking about me. "Haley?"

My tongue hurts. My head does too.

What's going on? I ask, but no one answers me.

"She's trying to speak."

I see. I need to move my lips for them to hear me. "What happened?" I force the sound out of my mouth, but it comes out slurred. Open my eyes. There's a bright lamp smack behind someone's head, someone looking down at me. I have no idea who this is. He's a big dark shape with a halo around his head.

"You had another seizure, honey." A new voice is deep and rich, a voice that makes my heart soar, makes me feel five years old. Am I five years old? He moves into my line of vision next to the other hulking shape.

"Dad?"

He smiles—"Hi, honey"—and runs his fingers through my hair with one hand, the other holding his phone to his ear. "She's awake. It's okay, Jen. I'll call you when we leave. Yeah, I'm going to give it to her right now."

Wait, he's talking to Mom. But he spoke so casually to her. On the phone. Usually they have text wars, furious fingers flying. Why so nice? I try to sit up.

"Whoa, take it easy there," he says, holding my arm steady. He hands me a pill with a glass of water. "Here. Take your Tegretol."

I take it and drink from the glass. I end up drinking the entire glass of water. *Holy crap, thirsty.* "Are you and Mom . . ." Together? I want to ask. But they're divorced, aren't they? Oh man, I'm so confused. Suddenly snippets of memories flash through my mind, fragments flying around and piecing themselves together. I sit up straight and stare at my dad in horror.

Fort Wilderness. Nineteen eighty-two.

I was there. He was there. A boy named Jason. Did I succeed in keeping my parents together?

Except that means . . . What about Alice and Willy? Without my future stepmom, do they even exist? Did I just succeed in making sure they're never born? My head drops into my hands. "Oh, God, what have I done?"

"It's okay, baby." My dad holds both my arms and peers into my face. "You haven't done anything. Your mom and I are fine."

I look up, eyebrows twisting on my forehead. "So you guys are still married?" Now I won't have my little brother and sister. Oh my God, what was I thinking? I look around. A few faces stare back at me. One of them is familiar, but I can't tell who it is. The other . . . is Erica.

Erica? What's she doing here if my parents are together? She smiles at me and wiggles her fingers. "Hey, you."

My dad glances at Erica, then at me again. I'm confused, and they're trying to help me. "No, honey. Your mom is in Jupiter. We're not married anymore." He and Erica chuckle. "I was just letting her know you're okay. She was worried about you."

Oh.

So they're still divorced? I didn't make them stay together forever? So it *was* fate? There was nothing I could do to change the outcome. But they were so friendly on the phone to each other just now, something *I've* never seen before. Did I do that? With my love-at-first-sight experiment? Did I ensure that even after splitting, they would always have a fondness for each other?

Well, that's definitely an improvement. I'll take it. "It was all a dream?"

Dad's eyebrows twist in confusion. He and Erica exchange lots of silent glances. "Haley, what are you talking about?"

"My little brother and sister?" I ask, looking around. "Where are they?"

"They're outside. On the rocking chairs."

"Rocking chairs," I reply. Why can't I put it all together? So frustrating!

"Yes, at Pioneer Hall. We're in Fort Wilderness. We came on vacation, remember? But you apparently went trespassing last night, like the mother's child that you are, and lost consciousness back there in River Country. It's the next day. About dinnertime."

I look at Erica. "I made you miss the Magic Kingdom," I mumble.

"It's okay, Haley. We're just glad you're okay," Erica says.

So it *was* a dream. Everything had happened in my mind. I just fell and dreamed it all. I'd be lying if I didn't say how excruciatingly disappointed that makes me.

"This man right here found you." Dad points to the other guy blocking the light.

He steps out of the glare and smiles at me. I half recognize him. His brown eyes are dark, eyebrows heavy. There's gray around his temples, and I cannot, for the life of me, say where I've seen him before.

"Thanks again, old buddy." My dad claps him on the shoulder. They know each other. Yes, I've seen him before. He's rescued me before.

"Not a problem, Oscar."

Wait. He's rescued me before?!

"Do I need to sign any release forms, Jake? I'll take her straight to the Orange County Hospital from here."

"Jake?" I stare at him.

No way! He doesn't have a mustache, and he's not wearing shorts

223

that are too small for him, but he's old, like my dad, and he's giving me a very, very cautious look, like I shouldn't call him Jake or let on that I know him. But *ohmigosh*, it's Jake! It wasn't a dream! It was real!

A flood of dream memories charges into my mind, like when he was looking down at me as I lay on the beach in River Country, making sure I was okay. The moment I met his brother, Jason, the glowing blond hairs on his arm, the fireworks, the Marshmallow Marsh . . .

Jake laughs nervously, looking up at my dad. "Can I speak to your daughter alone? I need to go over some safety rules that we expect from our guests here at Fort Wilderness. It's just a formality, buddy. I'll let her go in a minute."

Wary looks from my dad, but he signals for Erica to come outside with him. "Yeah, sure. We'll be right outside." For a moment, I hear Willy and Alice crying, "Daddy!" Then he closes the door behind him, and it's only me and Jake.

A slow smile spreads on his face. "Hello, Haley."

"Jake! Where's your brother? Is he here? Oh my God, he's here? How old is he? Oh my God, this is freaking me out." I want to see him. I want to see him, until I realize he wouldn't be the same exact person anymore. Sort of, but different. And way older.

"Relax, Haley. He's not here."

"Oh."

What does that mean? Is he dead? He died in the army, didn't he? I cover my face with my hands and take a deep breath in.

"He's in Glendale. California. At WDI."

Glendale, California.

I uncover my face. "What's WDI?" I ask, my voice unsteady.

"Imagineering. He's an engineer for Disney." He must see the look of utter shock, confusion, relief, and holy-crap happiness on my face, because he clarifies as much as he can, for the utterly stupid person I am right now. "He works for Disney, hon, just like I do. Except I'm here, and he's there. We got through some hard times because of this place. We owe them."

I haven't cried in years. Then I cried when I left Jason. And now I'm crying again. "He's an engineer for Disney. . . ." My voice trails off, and my hands cover my face again. "That is so nice to hear, Jake. Oh my God. *So* nice to hear." My eyes leak, wetting my hands and cheeks. I wipe the tears away.

His hand closes over my shoulder, and I don't know why, but this makes me sob harder. I look up at him, and he smiles sadly. Now I see it. The twenty-year-old Jake there, right in his cheeks. "Yeah. I was worried about him too."

"What does he do for them? Engineer what?"

"Ride designs. Rock 'n' Roller Coaster, for one." He tilts his head and waits for me to think about that.

And . . . I think I'm going to pass out again. There's too many emotions going on, and I don't feel well. So, the love of my life, who is now too old for me, who lived on without me, made it through his hard times without me, created my *favorite ride* of all the rides at Disney World? I . . . I can't think of anything more sad but awesome right now.

"That's my favorite ride," I laugh-cry at the same time.

"Is it?" he says, half like he's asking and half like he already knew. "What else can you tell me?"

He sighs and leans back against a counter. "I knew you were going to fall out of the darkness, like you appeared out of nowhere thirty-some years ago. The first week of July. So I've been out here this whole week, waiting for you."

"Are *you* the one who was following me when I broke into River Country?"

"Yep."

Suddenly I remember the other kids. God, what were their names? "These kids . . . that I was with before I slipped in time . . . they said there's a troll in River Country. Was that you?"

He laughs, his shoulders shuddering when he does. "Yeah, that's what I tell my daughter and the kids here when they stay for the summer. To keep them out of the back. It's illegal, you know. Troll," he says again and chuckles. "Wait, you met my daughter?"

"Um, I think. What's your daughter's name again?"

"Dina. You remember Marsha, right?" His face lights up and he checks back at the door, I guess to make sure my dad can't hear our conversation. *How could I forget? I just saw her yesterday, Jake.* "Well, that's us. Dina's our daughter."

"I am just . . . oh, God. This is all just amazing. It's distressing but amazing. But what about Jason? Why isn't he here? If he knew when I was coming back, why didn't he come?"

At this, he presses his lips together and just blinks a couple of times. "It's better this way, Haley. Don't you think so? I mean, he's an old guy now. You wouldn't want to see him that way." He's not asking how I'd feel about it. He's telling me, reminding, warning . . . that this is the way to go.

I guess he's right. Maybe. I mean, just a few minutes ago I was with him. A fog is clearing away now, and the memory of his arms, his kiss, slowly creeps back into my mind. I don't answer, just look down at my hands.

Now is when I notice that I'm on a couch in an office. Outside the window, I see the boats that take passengers to the Magic Kingdom. "What day is it?"

"July fourth, 2014."

"So it's the day after I seized?" I ask. It was July 4 when I left 1982. I guess I lose days when I travel backward but stay on the same day when I move forward. I wonder if this will ever happen again. If it does, I'll figure the logistics out.

Jake nods. "Yup. It's been a little less than twenty-four hours. I found you, looked up the only Petersen staying here, and found it was your dad. We've been waiting for you to wake up all day. Just in time for fireworks." He crosses his arms and leans back against the table. "Life is weird, Haley. Really weird."

"You're not kidding." I rub my forehead.

"Hey. I want to tell you something." He takes a deep breath, clasps his hands between his knees. "You told me I didn't have to be a jerk once. I'll never forget that. I don't know why, but that really stung me. Because of you, I didn't lose Marsha. She should have left me." He laughs, shaking his shoulders again. He looks back up at me. "But she didn't."

"I thought she liked Jason better."

"She did, but I fought for her."

"Wow." I smile. "Then I'm glad for you."

"Me too. So listen, two things . . . I'm going to go out there now and tell your dad that he needs to go to the main registration building and sign some papers while you rest here for a bit."

"Okay." This sounds like a plan in action—a secret plan. *I like it.*

"And after he leaves, I'm going to take you somewhere for a minute. You have to promise . . . swear, Haley . . . that you won't tell anyone, okay?"

"Okay."

"Promise me."

"I promise."

"Good, 'cause I could get into serious trouble for it." The Boy Scout is back. Same Jake as always. Way older, a little thicker, still handsome, and still afraid of getting in trouble. Some things never change.

"I said I promise."

"All right then, let's go." He gets up and stretches, talking over his shoulder. His hand pauses on the doorknob. "Lie down, like you were before."

"Right, okay." I lie down.

He opens the door and goes outside, leaving the door ajar, and I can hear him telling my dad and Erica everything he said he would.

My dad sounds a bit hesitant and peers into the room to look at me, but I wave at him, and he seems relieved.

Willy pokes his head into the room. "Hi, Tataaaa!"

"Hi!" I wave at him and fight back tears of gratitude that I did not change the course of his existence. He's my brother, and he's too cute not to live, so I'm okay—*so* okay—with the way things turned out. I'm fine with it, really.

"Thanks, man. Okay. Be back in a bit," my dad says outside the door. "Sorry for all the trouble."

"No trouble at all, not at all!" Jake smiles. Once my dad takes off in the golf cart, the one I drove on the night I fell into River Country, which technically was last night, but to me was eons ago, Jake calls me over to the door. I stand and wait a moment to make sure I can walk. "You feel okay?"

"Yeah, I'm better."

"Good." Jake opens a cabinet and pulls out a pair of lost-and-found flip-flops, tossing them on the floor under my feet. I guess I left mine in 1982. He clasps me on the shoulder and leads me onto the side porch of Pioneer Hall, where his office is. I remember now Dina telling me her dad was the manager here. Four kids are sitting outside, and they all stand up when they see us emerge.

One of them is Dina. She's wearing exactly what she was wearing when I last saw her, whereas I'm in my shorts and one of Jason's mom's shirts. She looks relieved and, wow, just like her mom! I want to tell her that her mother is beautiful and so very sweet.

"Hey, you. I was really worried," she says smiling a big, bright smile.

"Thanks. Sorry I scared you. I should've told you that these things sometimes happen to me." I smile, reaching out and touching her on the shoulder. I must've really freaked her out when I left her alone and swam into River Country like a Navy SEAL.

"It's okay. I'm sorry you're in trouble. Dad, this is totally my fault. We were playing scavenger hunt, and I told her to go in there and take photos of River Country. It was stupid of me. Please don't report her."

Jake takes on a new-to-me fatherly and managerial tone. "I'll see, Dina. But this is a serious offense."

"Dad, please."

"So you already met my intrepid daughter." Jake sighs at his daughter, ignoring her, like he'll think about it. It's nice to be on the inside of a joke for once. "And these guys are Rudy and Marcus, who stay here every summer—"

"Whom I also met," I interrupt. "Hey, guys." It feels like forever, *forever*, since I saw all them. But there's one more, and I don't know who it is.

Until he steps in closer, and my heart stops beating. Like literally stops, and I think I'm going to either have a heart attack or a seizure one more time. *Jason?* But that's impossible. How can it be? Jason is like fifty years old right now and in California.

"And, Haley . . ." Jake gets behind the Jason look-alike, who has to be my same age, around seventeen, eighteen, and holds him by the shoulders. He gives me a special look in the dimness of the porch, almost like he's given this premeditated thought and understands how seeing this guy might affect me. "This is my son, Ethan."

twenty-three

Not Jason.

But Jason's nephew.

I don't know why, but I'm so disheartened, I want to cry again. I know he couldn't have followed me into the future, but still—I wish I could see him again. I also wonder if Jason has any kids of his own. I guess it would all hurt less if I just don't ask.

Ethan smiles at me, and my heart splinters into a million pieces inside my chest. His smile is crooked, his eyebrows drawn together, his eyes—sparkling deep blue, just like his uncle's. "Hey," he says with a wave.

"Hey." *Breathe, Haley, breeeeathe. Do not cry.*

Jake knows how much his son looks like his brother. He knows what it's doing to me. I see it in his sympathetic look. Luckily, he cuts the awkward moment short. "Guys, we'll see you all later. I have to take Haley to the main gate."

"Does she have to leave?" Dina asks, keeping up the pace with her father. I finally tear my gaze away from the Jason look-alike. It hurts me that I will never get to see Jason that young ever again. And here's what I think—no, *know*—maybe meeting Ethan was the universe's way of giving me one last look at him.

"I won't report it. If she leaves, that's up to her father." Jake turns to me. "Let's go, young lady."

"Bye, guys. Maybe I'll see you later," I tell them, because I'll probably get my original wish now and go home to Jupiter, even though I don't want to leave anymore. I love this place. I want to come every year, maybe even stay the whole summer.

As Dina, Rudy, and Marcus walk away, I can hear the boys talking. "So who won the scavenger hunt?"

"I guess it was us," Marcus says. "Ha-ha, suckers."

"Shut up," Dina blurts, and I could kill myself. Kill myself! I have—had—the River Country photos on my phone, but I lost them. That was item number two! Well, I should consider myself lucky that I even landed back in the same time and place in one piece. Forget the phone.

Jake and I climb into his mac-daddy golf cart, an official Disney one with nice leather seats and room for like eight people. He pulls out his phone and fires off random texts. "I'm waiting for them to leave."

"Ah. Got it."

"By the way, thanks for the tip. We all bought stock in these babies." He lifts his iPhone slightly and smiles a slick smile without looking up.

"Oh, wow," I say. "That is just . . . awesome. I lost mine, you know." I stare down the driveway. The driveway facing River Country. The same place I stopped and stared into the darkness and that great iron wall blocking it from view.

"I know," Jake mumbles.

It's there. River Country is there. I see it clearly in my mind, both as a shining, active hubbub under the blazing Florida sun and as an overgrown, reclaimed patch of swamp. It was a great water park. I'll give my dad that. And I saw it with my own eyes.

Suddenly we're zooming past Pioneer Hall, but our drive is short. He parks in a small lot right next to the marina. I hung out here with Jason just a couple of days ago and talked about Christopher Atkins, when he brought me food. "This is where we had what I guess you could call our first date. Right here," I tell Jake, and he smiles quietly and watches my face.

Then he sighs heavily, like it was so long ago. But for me, it's fresh. Too fresh. He leads me down the marina, talks to a cast member in the rental office, and takes a key from him. "Thanks, Quin. Come on, Haley."

"Where are we going?" I ask, but right away I think I know. The only other time Jake took me on a small boat ride from the Fort Wilderness Marina, it was to that little island out in the darkness, the one that's going to hold a lot of bittersweet memories for me from now until the day I die.

"You know where."

I do. And I let him take me. Only this time the island is shrouded in darkness. I'm not sure I want to go there and stir anything up. What lives there now is beyond me. We get into a small boat, bigger than a speedboat, and I sit and watch Jake expertly engage the engine and maneuver his way out of the marina.

There's a good-size crowd on the beach, but there're no bonfires. Everyone is waiting for the fireworks to begin. I know the beauty of the night over Bay Lake. I lived it firsthand. And it saddens me that these people are not seeing it with a water parade after the Marshmallow Marsh canoe ride like I did.

Jake and I are silent. We reach Discovery Island, and for a minute we sit there in the pure darkness of the lake, staring at it. It's black in there and awfully quiet. There's no dock anymore. The waves around us lap quietly against the side of the boat. He urges the boat on suddenly so that it circles the island from the north over to the west side, and there he runs it aground on the shore.

Jake gets out of the craft, pulls it forward as much as he can using the rope tied to the front, reaches into the boat, and pulls out a strong Maglite. He holds out his hand for me. I take it and carefully step out onto the sand. "Why are we here?"

I follow him down the beach. This is it. This is the same place I was earlier today. It is the weirdest feeling to see a huge passage of time on a beautiful place, to see it deteriorating out in the middle of the lake, abandoned and forlorn, when it was magical only hours before. "He told me to bring you here."

Jason.

Jason told his brother to bring me here if he ever found me. "Why?" In the beam of his flashlight, I see there's no *Walrus* anymore, no shed. From here I can still see the concrete structures, the cages and pens that held the animals of this reserve thirty-two years ago when I was there today, but nothing now. Oddly enough, I now see one lamp light on in the middle of the island.

"How come that light still works?"

"Oh, this whole place still has full electricity. So does River Country. It's all networked with Pioneer Hall. When they built this whole part of the campground, they never imagined some sections of it would close in the future." So even abandoned River Country still has power? No wonder I heard creepy music when I wandered in there.

"Why did River Country close?" I ask.

"Don't know for sure." He stops in the sand, one hand on his hip, the other lighting up the ground around us. "River Country used the natural lake. They always used bromine to keep it clean. But I think there was a movement to only have municipal water at water parks," he says. "Or maybe it's just that they couldn't compete with all the newer water parks."

And suddenly I know where we are going.

We trudge through the sand that is dirty and overgrown with tall grasses to a spot, and I almost don't want to go inside, but he points his flashlight into a break in the rocks, and even from here I can hear the water running.

I cover my face with my hands and shake my head. "I can't."

"Haley." He pulls my hand away and makes me look at him. "I've waited thirty-two years to bring you here, so you are most definitely going in there." He smiles. "Come on, I'll go with you."

He goes in first, then reaches back to take me by the hand. This is where we hid away from the world, where we could forget that anyone was chasing us and just be ourselves. I wonder if Jason thinks about that day (today!) like I always will. I would imagine that for him it's faded by now. Lucky him. I have to live with the memory brand-spanking-new on my mind until it leaves me, too.

If it ever does.

Haley Falls is still beautiful. Hidden and beautiful, and I wonder if anyone ever spent time in here after we did. Jake comes over to a rock and kicks it with the side of his shoe. "See this?"

"It's a rock."

"It's a fake rock, taken from River Country. Lift it."

"Okay." For real? His flashlight shines on it, and I bend down to move it. It's a little heavy, but not as heavy as a real rock that size would be. It feels stuck at first, but then it pulls away from the ground when I lift it, leaving its oblong imprint on the sand. It's hollow. Completely hollow. The perfect place to hide something, like those fake garden rocks for hiding your front door keys.

Inside, there's a bag.

A big plastic bag with a piece of yellowish paper inside and HALEY-HALEY written on it. A small muffled noise comes out of me. My head drops into my hands. I can't. I can't do this.

I feel Jake's hand on my shoulder. "It's okay."

"How long has this been here?" I whisper.

"A long time. But I come out here every so often, just to make sure it's still here. I also added something you're gonna need."

"What do you mean?" I pinch my nose and sniffle.

"Just open it. Here, take the flashlight. I'll wait outside." He hands me the Maglite, and it feels so heavy, or maybe I'm so weak. I take it and let its weight pull me down to the ground. I sit there for a minute, taking it all in.

Where I am.

What I'm doing.

How much everything has changed in such a short time.

I'll always be grateful for this hideaway. But I don't think I could ever come here again after this. Haley Falls will live on only in my memory. So I close my eyes and try to enjoy it one last time. I take a deep breath and take the bag from inside the rock.

Here goes nothing.

I set the flashlight at an angle so it keeps the bag illuminated, then I unzip the top. The first thing I take out is the note. I unfold it and bring it into the light. I let out a ginormous breath of air. It reads:

Dear Haley-Haley,

Don't know if you'll ever come back and find this, but hey, I have nothing to lose by trying.

right? You said that in the future, almost no one writes letters anymore. Well, it's not really the future for me yet, so here I am, writing a letter to you six years after I last saw you, because I want you to know something — I haven't forgotten you and never will. I don't know if I'll ever see you again, but you need to know that I owe everything I have to you. <u>Everything</u>. And you have to know that even if we never see each other again, that's OKAY. What's meant to happen will happen. And if it doesn't, it wasn't meant to be.

You're living on in my heart, Haley, like I hope I'll live on in yours.

I'll love you always,
Jason-Jason
7-4-88

I drop the note into my lap and close my eyes. He has the most beautiful handwriting I've ever seen from a boy. Okay, that hurts. Learning that about him now, and knowing there're a multitude of other things about him I'll never get to learn.

I wish I would've had more time. I wish I could've brought him back with me. I wish I wouldn't have focused so much on trying to get home and just spent my time and energy getting to know him. *I wish, I wish, I wish.*

I unfold the last quarter of the paper and there's more:

P.S. Keep the chain. I was going to give it to you that night and never got the chance.

I reach into the bag, and two more items slide out into my hand. One is his chain. His tacky gold chain with the rope twists that I made fun of. Now it's mine forever. The treasure on Discovery Island doesn't exist? The one from the scavenger hunt list? "Ha!" A crazy laugh escapes me, the kind that only happens when you truly let go, hysterics through tears.

And the other item—fits like a glove. White with white case. Cracked in the corner of the screen. My phone. Amazing. More proof that this wasn't all a dream. He found it here after I left it by accident. It's traveled thirty years back in time, then thirty years forward again. Now it's right back where it started. This sucker's seen more than I have.

He could've just kept it. My souvenir to him. I would've bought another one.

But then I remember the pics from River Country. Yes! Hopefully, they're still inside. Then I definitely won that scavenger hunt, hands down! I press the power button, but it doesn't turn on. I hear Jake's voice low along the ground. "Plug in the battery pack." I almost forgot about him. Has he been sitting there watching me this whole time? I guess he deserves it after waiting for me for so long. Or maybe he wants to tell his brother how I reacted when seeing it all.

Inside the bag is a battery pack, that old kind that you plug into the charging slot. I slide it into place and wait. As I sit there in the darkness, listening to the water run and the crickets chirp throughout the island, another sound joins the night, one I'm familiar with, one that will never mean the same without Jason.

Fireworks from Magic Kingdom.

Like clockwork every night.

And they'll be extra special tonight.

I look up and smile as the first big explosion of sparkles fizzles into the horizon of trees. My phone turns on right then. First the battery symbol, then the glowing apple, and finally . . .

Oh my God.

While we were sitting and playing with my phone, after we hot-wired it, I guess, he took a picture of us. My head on his shoulder, a giddy smile on my face and on his—amazement, upon discovering technology beyond his wildest dreams. It's serene and content, a moment in time that I'll never have again. It even has an ethereal hazy glow you can't get with any photo-editing app.

And he set it as my home screen.

So it'd be the first thing I saw when I got my phone back.

"Rad, Jason." I can't help but smile from ear to ear.

Never will I *ever* change this pic.

All I wanted this summer was a fling, but instead I got Jason. Love in River Country, of all places. A huge teardrop slides off my nose and lands smack right in the middle of our pic, splattering out in all directions, light from the screen filtering through the tear, creating a myriad of colors. Like shimmery, dreamy fireworks at the end of a long, magical day.

acknowledgments

I was doing a last-minute check of my laptop's trash one day when I opened a story I'd started over a year before. I'd only written a few chapters and didn't know what to do with it anymore, and being the hater of clutter than I am, I had tossed it. But then I gave it one last read, and something stopped me. How could I throw out a story set in Disney World, my favorite place in the world, during the eighties, the time I grew up? I'd make it work somehow. I *had* to finish it! Those chapters turned into *Summer of Yesterday*, a love letter to a place and time forever etched into my heart.

Like Haley, there are people in our lives who believe in us. Like Jason, they risk a lot to support us. But those who bring us down are important as well. They give our lives obstacles, conflict, so our victories can be sweeter. So I'd like to thank *everyone* who played a part in getting this book out. To the one who said, "She won't succeed," thank you for pissing me off, making me want to win even more. To the one who said, "She doesn't have what it takes," thank you for forcing me to work harder. To the one who said, "I don't believe in her," thank you for helping me find angels who do. But mostly, thanks to my children—Noah, Murphy, and Michael—for keeping me focused and filling my life with purpose; my mother, Yolanda, for being the only person who read the entire draft when the world was too busy; my father, Oscar, for taking me to Fort Wilderness when I was little and shooting video of River Country and the train that's no longer there; SCBWI Florida, my thirteen-year-long support system; my editor, Patrick Price, for understanding how important this story was to me and for fighting for it; my amazing agent, Deborah Warren, for taking a risk and believing in me when I needed it most.

Without these "folks," a new generation would never know about River Country, an awesome, forgotten place in time. But most of all, my husband, Chris, who's always said, "Don't worry about anything . . . just write." You have no idea how important that was to me. Thank you all from the bottom of my heart.

about the author

GABY TRIANA is the author of many books for young adults, a cake designer, a mother of three boys, and an all-around extremely busy person. Her books include *Backstage Pass*, *Cubanita*, *The Temptress Four*, and *Riding the Universe*, which collectively have earned an IRA Teen Choice Award; been listed as ALA Best Paperbacks; been praised by *Booklist*, *School Library Journal*, *Kliatt*, *Kirkus*, and *Publishers Weekly*; and been named one of *Hispanic* magazine's Good Reads of 2008. In addition to writing books and designing whimsical, sculpted cakes, Gaby serves as Co-Regional Advisor for SCBWI Florida. Her obsessions include Disney World, Halloween, "The Legend of Sleepy Hollow," driving fast cars, planning writing conferences, and spending time with her family in Miami. Visit her at www.gabytriana.com.

Want some more summer romance?

Read on for a peek at

Pulled Under,

a Sixteenth Summer novel,

by Michelle Dalton.

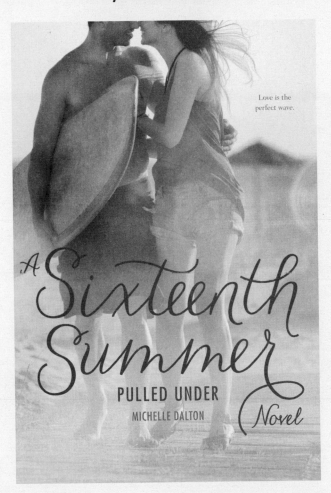

*D*ifficult questions come in all shapes and sizes. They can be big and philosophical, like "What's the meaning of life?" Or small and personal, like "How do you know if you're really in love?" They can even be evil (Yes, I'm talking about you, Mrs. Perkins), like "For the quadratic equation where the equation has only one solution, what's the value of C?" But of all the world's questions there is one that stands alone as the single most difficult to answer.

"Does this bathing suit make me look fat?"

If you've ever been asked, then you know what I'm talking about. It's not like you can just say, "No, but your butt kinda does." And it's not like you can say, "Oh no, it looks great. You should definitely wear that on the beach, where every guy you know will see you." Instead you have to find that delicate place between honesty and kindness.

I know this because I hear the question all the time. I work weekends and summers at Surf Sisters, a surf shop in Pearl Beach, Florida, where women asking you how they look in all varieties of swimwear kind of comes with the turf. (Or as my father would say, it "comes with the *surf*," because, you know, dads.)

It's been my experience that a great many of those who ask the question already know the answer. This group includes the girls with the hot bodies who only ask because they want to hear someone say how great they look. My response to them is usually just to shrug and answer, "It doesn't make you look fat, but it is kind of strange for your torso." The proximity of the words "strange" and "torso" in the same sentence usually keeps them from asking again.

Most girls, however, ask because while they know a swimsuit doesn't look right, they're not exactly sure why. That's the case with the girl who's asking me right now. All she wants is to look her best and to feel good about herself. Unfortunately, the bikini she's trying on is preventing that from happening. My first step is to help her get rid of *it* for reasons that have nothing to do with *her*.

"I think it looks good on you," I answer. "But I don't love what happens with that particular swimsuit when it gets wet. It loses its shape and it starts to look dingy."

"Really?" she says. "That's not good."

I sense that she's relieved to have an excuse to get rid of it, so I decide to wade deeper into the waters of truthfulness. "And, to be honest, it doesn't seem like you feel very comfortable in it."

She looks at me and then she looks at herself in the mirror and shakes her head. "No, I don't, do I? I'm no good at finding the right suit."

"Luckily, I can help you with that," I say. "But I need to know what you're looking for, and I need to know how you see yourself. Are you a shark or a dolphin?"

She cocks her head to the side. "What do you mean?"

"Sharks are sleek and deadly. They're man-eaters."

"And dolphins?"

"They're more . . . playful and intelligent."

She thinks it over for a moment and smiles. "Well, I probably wish I was more of a shark, but . . . I'm a total dolphin."

"So am I. You know, in the ocean, if a shark and a dolphin fight, the dolphin always wins."

"Maybe, but on land it usually goes the other way."

We both laugh, and I can tell that I like her.

"Let's see what we can do about that," I say. "I think we've got a couple styles that just might help a dolphin out."

Fifteen minutes later, when I'm ringing her up at the register, she is happy and confident. I know it sounds hokey, but this is what I love about Surf Sisters. Unlike most shops, where girls have to be bikini babes or they're out of luck, this one has always been owned and operated by women. And while we have plenty of male customers, we've always lived by the slogan, "Where the waves meet the curves."

At the moment it also happens to be where the waves meet the pouring rain. That's why, when my girl leaves with not one but two new and empowering swimsuits, the in-store population of employees outnumbers customers three to two. And, since both customers seem more interested in waiting out the storm than in buying anything, I'm free to turn my attention to the always entertaining *Nicole and Sophie Show*.

"You have no idea what you're talking about," Nicole says as they expertly fold and stack a new display of T-shirts. "Absolutely. No. Idea."

In addition to being my coworkers, Nicole and Sophie have been my best friends for as long as I can remember. At first glance they seem like polar opposites. Nicole is a blue-eyed blonde who stands six feet tall, most of which is arms and legs. This comes in handy as heck on the volleyball court but makes her self-conscious when it comes to boys. Sophie, meanwhile, is petite and fiery. She's half Italian, half Cuban, all confidence.

Judging by Nic's signature blend of outrage and indignation, Sophie must be offering unsolicited opinions in regard to her terminal crush on the oh-so-cute but always-out-of-reach Cody Bell.

"There was a time when it was an embarrassing but still technically acceptable infatuation," Sophie explains. "But that was back around ninth-grade band camp. It has since gone through various stages of awkward, and I'm afraid can now only be described as intervention-worthy stalking."

Although I've witnessed many versions of this exact conversation over the years, this is the first time I've seen it in a while. That's because Sophie just got back from her freshman year at college. Watching them now is like seeing the season premiere of a favorite television show. Except without the microwave popcorn.

"Stalking?" Nicole replies. "Do you know how absurd that sounds?"

"No, but I do know how absurd it *looks*," Sophie retorts. "You go wherever he goes, but you never talk to him. Or if you do talk to him, it's never about anything real, like the fact that you're into him."

"Where are you even getting your information?" Nicole demands. "You've been two hundred miles away. For all you know, Cody and I had a mad, passionate relationship while you were away at Florida State."

Sophie turns to me and rolls her eyes. "Izzy, were there any mad, passionate developments in the Nicole and Cody saga while I was in Tallahassee? Did they become a supercouple? Did the celebrity press start referring to them as 'Nicody'?"

I'm not about to lie and say that there were new developments, but I also won't throw Nicole under the bus and admit that the situation has actually gotten a little worse. Instead, I take the coward's way out.

"I'm Switzerland," I say. "Totally neutral and all about the chocolate."

"Your courage is inspiring," mocks Sophie before directing the question back at Nicole. "Then you tell me. Did you have a mad, passionate relationship with Cody this year?"

"No," Nicole admits after some hesitation. "I was just pointing out that you weren't here, so you have no way of knowing what did or did not happen."

"So you're saying you did not follow him around?"

"Cody and I have some similar interests and are therefore occasionally in the same general vicinity. But that doesn't mean that I follow him around or that it's developed into . . . whatever it was that you called it."

"Intervention-worthy stalking," I interject.

Nicole looks my way and asks, "How exactly do you define 'neutral'?"

I mimic locking my mouth shut with a key and flash a cheesy apology grin.

"So it's not because of Cody that you suddenly decided that you wanted to switch to the drum line?" Sophie asks. "Even though you've been first-chair clarinet for your entire life?"

"You told her about drum line?" Nicole says, giving me another look.

"You're gonna be marching at football games in front of the entire town," I say incredulously. "It's not exactly top secret information."

"I changed instruments because I wanted to push myself musically," Nicole explains. "The fact that Cody is also on the drum line is pure coincidence."

"Just like it's coincidence that Cody is the president of Latin Club and you're the newly elected vice president?"

Another look at me. "Seriously?"

"I was proud of you," I say, trying to put a positive spin on it. "I was bragging."

"Yes, it's a coincidence," she says, turning back to Sophie. "By the way, there are plenty of girls in Latin Club and I don't see you accusing any of them of stalking."

"First of all, there aren't *plenty* of girls in Latin Club. I bet there are like *three* of them," Sophie counters. "And unlike you, I'm sure they actually take Latin. You take Spanish, which means that you should be in—what's it called again?—oh yeah, Spanish Club."

It's worth pointing out that despite her time away, Sophie is not the least bit rusty. She's bringing her A game, and while it might sound harsh to outsiders, trust me when I say this is all being done out of love.

"I had a scheduling conflict with Spanish Club," Nicole offers. "Besides, I thought Latin Club would look good on my college applications."

It's obvious that no matter how many examples Sophie provides, Nicole is going to keep dodging the issue with lame excuse after lame excuse. So Sophie decides to go straight to the finish line. Unfortunately, I'm the finish line.

"Sorry, Switzerland," she says. "This one's on you. Who's right? Me or the Latin drummer girl?"

Before you jump to any conclusions, let me assure you that she's not asking because I'm some sort of expert when it comes to boys. In fact, both of them know that I have virtually zero firsthand experience. It's just that I'm working the register, and whenever there's a disagreement at the shop, whoever's working the register breaks the tie. This is a time-honored tradition, and at Surf Sisters we don't take traditions lightly.

"You're really taking it to the register?" I ask, wanting no part of this decision. "On your first day back?"

"I really am," Sophie answers, giving me no wiggle room.

"Okay," I say to her. "But in order for me to reach a verdict, you'll have to explain why it is that you've brought this up now. Except for Latin Club, all the stuff you're talking about is old news."

"First of all, I've been away and thought you were keeping an eye on her," she says. "And it's not old. While you were helping that girl find a swimsuit—awesome job, by the way . . ."

"Thank you."

". . . Nicole was telling me about last week when she spent two hours following Cody from just a few feet away. She followed him in and out of multiple buildings, walked when he walked, stopped when he stopped, and never said a single word to him. That's textbook stalking."

"Okay. Wow," I reply, a little surprised. "That does sound . . . really bad. Nicole?"

"It only sounds bad because she's leaving out the part about us being on a campus tour at the University of Florida," Nicole says with a spark of attitude. "And the part about there being fifteen people in the group, all of whom were stopping and walking together in and out of buildings. And the fact that we *couldn't* talk because we were listening to the tour guide, and nothing looks worse to an admissions counselor than hitting on someone when you're supposed to be paying attention."

I do my best judge impression as I point an angry finger at Sophie. "Counselor, I am tempted to declare a mistrial as I believe you have withheld key evidence."

"Those are minor details," she scoffs. "It's still stalking."

"Besides, you have your facts wrong," I continue. "It wasn't last week. Nicole visited UF over a month ago, which puts it outside the statute of limitations."

It's at this moment that I notice the slightest hint of a guilty expression on Nicole's face. It's only there for a second, but it's long enough for me to pause.

"I thought you said it was last week," Sophie says to her.

Nicole clears her throat for a moment and replies, "I don't see how it matters when it occurred."

"It matters," Sophie says.

"Besides," I add, also confused, "you told me all about that visit and you never once mentioned that Cody was there."

"Maybe because, despite these ridiculous allegations, I am not obsessed with him. I was checking out a college, not checking out a guy."

"Oh! My! God!" says Sophie, figuring it out. "You went back for a second visit, didn't you? You took the tour last month. Then you went back and took it again last week because you knew that Cody was going to be there and it would give you a reason to follow him around."

Nicole looks at both of us and, rather than deny the charge, she goes back to folding shirts. "I believe a mistrial was declared in my favor."

"Izzy only said she was *tempted* to declare one," Sophie says. "Besides, she never rang the register."

"I distinctly heard the register," Nicole claims.

"No, you didn't," I say. "Is she right? Did you drive two and a half hours to Gainesville, take a two-hour tour you'd already taken a month ago, and drive back home for two and a half hours, just so you could follow Cody around the campus?"

She is silent for a moment and then nods slowly. "Pretty much."

"I'm sorry, but you are guilty as charged," I say as I ring the bell of the register.

"I really was planning on talking to him this time," she says, deflated. "I worked out a whole speech on the drive over, and then when the time came . . . I just froze."

Sophie thinks this over for a moment. "That should be your sentence."

"What do you mean?" asks Nicole.

"You have been found guilty and your sentence should be that you *have* to talk to him. No backing out. No freezing. And it has to be a real conversation. It can't be about band or Latin Club."

"What if he wants to talk about band or Latin Club? What if he brings it up? Am I just supposed to ignore him?"

"It's summer vacation and we live at the beach," Sophie says. "If he wants to talk about band or Latin, then I think it's time you found a new crush."

Nicole nods her acceptance, and I make it official. "Nicole

Walker, you are hereby sentenced to have an actual conversation with Cody Bell sometime within the next . . . two weeks."

"Two weeks?" she protests. "I need at least a month so I can plan what I'm going to say and organize my—"

"Two weeks," I say, cutting her off.

She's about to make one more plea for leniency when the door flies open and a boy rushes in from the rain. He's tall, over six feet, has short-cropped hair, and judging by the embarrassed look on his face, made a much louder entrance than he intended.

"Sorry," he says to the three of us. There's an awkward pause for a moment before he asks, "Can I speak to whoever's in charge?"

Without missing a beat, Nicole and Sophie both point at me. I'm not really in charge, but they love putting me on the spot, and since it would be pointless to explain that they're insane, I just go with it.

"How can I help you?"

As he walks to the register I do a quick glance-over. The fact that he's our age and I've never seen him before makes me think he's from out of town. So does the way he's dressed. His tucked-in shirt, coach's shorts, and white socks pulled all the way up complete a look that is totally lacking in beach vibe. (It will also generate a truly brutal farmer's tan once the rain stops.) But he's wearing a polo with a Pearl Beach Parks and Recreation logo on it, which suggests he's local.

I'm trying to reconcile this, and maybe I'm also trying to figure out exactly how tall he is, when I notice that he's looking at me with an expectant expression. It takes me a moment to realize that my glance-over might have slightly crossed the border into a stare-at, during which I was so distracted that I apparently missed the part when he asked me a question. This would be an appropriate time to add that despite the dorkiness factor in the above description, there's more than a little bit of dreamy about him.

"Well . . . ?" he asks expectantly.

I smile at him. He smiles at me. The air is ripe with awkwardness. This is when a girl hopes her BFFs might jump to her rescue and keep her from completely embarrassing herself. Unfortunately, one of mine just came back from college looking to tease her little high school friends, and the other thinks I was too tough on her during the sentencing phase of our just completed mock trial. I quickly realize that I am on my own.

"I'm sorry, could you repeat that?"

"Which part?" he asks, with a crooked smile that is also alarmingly distracting.

When it becomes apparent that I don't have an answer, Sophie finally chimes in. "I think you should just call it a do-over and repeat the whole thing."

She stifles a laugh at my expense, but I ignore her so that I can focus on actually hearing him this go-round. I'm counting on the second time being the charm.

"Sure," he says. "I'm Ben with Parks and Recreation, and I'm going to businesses all over town to see if they'll put up this poster highlighting some of the events we have planned for summer."

He unzips his backpack and pulls out a poster that has a picture of the boardwalk above a calendar of events. "We've got a parade, fireworks for the Fourth of July, all kinds of cool stuff, and we want to get the word out."

This is the part when a noncrazy person would just take the poster, smile, and be done with it. But, apparently, I'm not a noncrazy person. So I look at him (again), wonder exactly how tall he is (again), and try to figure out who he is (again).

"I'm sorry, *who* are you?"

"Ben," he says slowly, and more than a little confused. "I've said that like three times now."

"No, I don't mean 'What's your name?' I mean 'Who are you?' Pearl Beach is not that big and I've lived here my whole life. How is it possible that you work at Parks and Rec and we've never met before?"

"Oh, that's easy," he says. "Today's my first day on the job. I'm visiting for the summer and staying with my uncle. I live in Madison, Wisconsin."

"Well," I hear Sophie whisper to Nicole, "that explains the socks."

Finally, I snap back to normalcy and smile. "It's nice to meet you, Ben from Wisconsin. My name's Izzy. Welcome to Pearl Beach."

Over the next few minutes, Ben and I make small talk while we hang the poster in the front window. I know hanging a poster might not seem like a two-person job, but this way one of us (Ben) can tape the poster up while the other (me) makes sure it's straight.

Unfortunately when I go outside to look in the window to

check the poster, I see my own reflection and I'm mortified. The rain has caused my hair to frizz in directions I did not think were possible, and I have what appears to be a heart-shaped guacamole stain on my shirt. (Beware the dangers of eating takeout from Mama Tacos in a cramped storeroom.) I try to nonchalantly cover the stain, but when I do it just seems like I'm saying the Pledge of Allegiance.

"How's that look?" he asks when I go back in.

I'm still thinking about my shirt, so I start to say "awful," but then realize he's talking about the poster he just hung, so I try to turn it into "awesome." It comes out somewhere in the middle, as "Awfslome."

"What?"

"Awesome," I say. "The poster looks awesome."

"Perfect. By the way, I'm about to get some lunch and I was wondering . . ."

Some psychotic part of me actually thinks he's just going to ask me out to lunch. Like that's something that happens. To me. It isn't.

". . . where'd you get the Mexican food?"

"The what?"

That's when he points at the stain on my shirt. "The guacamole got me thinking that Mexican would be *muy bueno* for lunch."

For a moment I consider balling up in the fetal position, but I manage to respond. "Mama Tacos, two blocks down the beach."

"*Gracias!*" he says with a wink. He slings the backpack over his shoulder, waves good-bye to the girls, and disappears back into the rain. Meanwhile, I take the long, sad walk back toward the register wondering how much Nicole and Sophie overheard.

"I noticed that stain earlier and meant to point it out," Nicole says.

"Thanks," I respond. "That might have been helpful."

"Well, I don't know about you guys," Sophie says. "But I think Ben is 'awfslome'!"

So apparently they heard every word.